Mário

Lúcio's Confession

Translated from the Portuguese
by Margaret Jull Costa and
with a foreword by
Dr Eugénio Lisboa

Dedalus

Dedalus would like to thank The Calouste Gulbenkian Foundation – London and Camões Institute – Lisbon for their assistance in producing this book.

Published by Dedalus Ltd, Langford Lodge, St Judith's Lane, Sawtry, Cambs, PE17 5XE

ISBN 1 873982 80 1

Distributed in Canada by Marginal Distribution,
Unit 103, 277, George Street North, Peterborough, Ontario, KJ9 3G9
Distributed in Australia & New Zealand by Peribo Pty Ltd,
26, Tepko Road, Terrey Hills, N.S.W. 2084

Publishing History
First published in Portugal in 1913
First English edition 1993

Typeset by Datix International, Bungay, Suffolk
Printed in Finland by Wsoy

A C.I.P. listing for this title is available on request.

DEDALUS EUROPE 1992–1995

Dedalus, as part of its Europe 1992–95 programme, with the assistance of the Calouste Gulbenkian Foundation in London and the Camões Institute in Lisbon, has embarked on a series of new translations by Margaret Jull Costa of some of the major classics of Portuguese literature.

Titles so far selected are:

Dedalus European Classics

The Mandarin (and other stories) – Eça de Queiroz

The Relic – Eça de Queiroz

Decadence from Dedalus

Lúcio's Confession – Mário de Sá-Carneiro

Short stories – Mário de Sá-Carneiro

Literary Fantasy Anthologies

The Dedalus Book of Portuguese Fantasy – editors Eugénio Lisboa and Helder Macedo

Further titles will be announced shortly.

To Sally & Jenny –
to say how much I
enjoyed your first
and hopefully not
your last visit to
Lisbon.
With lots of love
Richard
Christmas 1996

THE TRANSLATOR

Margaret Jull Costa has translated novels and short stories by Portuguese, Spanish and Latin American writers: among them are the Portuguese and Spanish stories in *The Dedalus Book of Surrealism*; *The Hero of the Big House* and *The Resemblance* by Alvaro Pombo; *The Last Days of William Shakespeare* by Vlady Kociancich; *The Witness* by Juan José Saer; *Obabakoak* by Bernardo Atxaga; *All Souls* by Javier Marías and *The Mandarin* by Eça de Queiroz.

She was joint-winner of the Portuguese Translation Prize in 1992 for her translation of *The Book of Disquiet* by Fernando Pessoa.

Her current projects include a collection of short stories by Mário de Sá-Carneiro, *The Relic* by Eça de Queiroz and *The Dedalus Book of Portuguese Fantasy*, edited by Eugénio Lisboa and Helder Macedo.

For António Ponce de Leão

. . . thus were we obscurely two, both of us unsure as to whether the other was not in fact himself, whether that uncertain other even existed . . .

Fernando Pessoa
(*In the Forest of Alienation*)

Foreword

The poet and fiction writer Mário de Sá-Carneiro was born in Lisbon in 1890 and committed suicide in Paris in 1916, when he was barely 26 years old. Although he did not leave a particularly large body of work, he was one of the most influential writers of what, in Portugal, is termed Primeiro Modernismo, its other major exponents being Fernando Pessoa (1888–1935) and Almada Negreiros (1893–1970). Mário de Sá-Carneiro has tended to be relegated to the background, very much in the shadow of Fernando Pessoa, but José Régio, the best-known representative of the literary movement that succeeded Primeiro Modernismo, had no hesitation in describing him – with some justification – as 'both the acknowledged forerunner and the greatest exponent of so-called Portuguese modernism'. Elsewhere, proving that his description of the author of *A confissão de Lúcio* (*Lúcio's Confession*) was not the product of some temporary aberration, Régio writes of Sá-Carneiro that he is 'one of our most remarkable poets' and 'the greatest interpreter of a particular contemporary sensibility'. Given that José Régio is generally considered to be one of Portugal's most penetrating *and* most cautious critics, his words have a certain weight.

Mário de Sá-Carneiro was, at once, one of the most strikingly innovative literary figures of his day and, intellectually, a typical child of the times: the years immediately preceding and including the First World War, with all the horrors that implies.

The future author of *Indícios de Ouro* (*Traces of Gold*) and *Céu em fogo* (*The Sky Ablaze*) was the rebellious son of an upper middle-class Lisbon family; he was also an erratic student, endowed with a bizarre and intense imagination. He tried studying law for a year at Coimbra University, then left for Paris where he enrolled in the same course, although without ever actually attending any lectures.

Sá-Carneiro was linked by ties of friendship and respect to Fernando Pessoa and the futurist group that grew up around the magazine *Orpheu* and, for a very brief period, he, like all his friends, found himself playing a part for which he had little natural inclination, that of *agent provocateur.* Sá-Carneiro was too honest, too *personal* to be involved for any length of time in rowdy burlesques, however well-intentioned, or to adhere to the conventions of any literary schools of thought, even those with which he was for some time associated: decadent symbolism, *paùlismo* (one of Fernando Pessoa's inventions), or noisy, superficial futurism . . . As Régio more than once remarked: 'in Mário de Sá-Carneiro the shaking up of worn-out formulae and antiquated means of expression . . . is a natural consequence of his anomalous poetic psyche'. Sá-Carneiro's way of living out his singular personality had an infectious intensity that transmitted itself to his readers. Like one of the characters in *Lúcio's Confession* he obliges his readers to be as intense as he is. And it is that very *intensity* which lends his strange confession its undeniable authenticity.

Sá-Carneiro shares another defect with certain of his characters, that of *excess*. Régio commented that for Sá-Carneiro: 'Shapes are sketchy outlines, lights mere glimmerings, memories vague recollections and images mirages – except when, paradoxically, all those things take on, in his eyes, an *unbearable, indeed excessive, intensity*.' That excess can be so overwhelming as to render us incapable of *absorbing* it. For that very reason, the poet writes elsewhere: 'I am dying of starvation, of excess': that is, having so much at my disposal, I am dying deprived of everything – excess paralyses and, eventually, kills.

This book, dated 1913, is a highly original work, closely connected to the profound and intense 'I' of Sá-Carneiro the poet. It is also a *dated* book, full of aesthetic mannerisms typical of the time. Dated or not, however, only a mischievously inattentive reader could fail to find in this remarkable work many of the perennial obsessions that pervade all the author's poetry and fiction: the feeling of abnormality, the mystery of madness, the paroxysmic experience of the senses, love, death and decadence. As Régio says: in *Lúcio's Confession*, as in Sá-Carneiro's other works of fiction, a story drenched in anomaly sometimes demands a deliberately academic prose, as a sort of antidote to all that anomalousness. Like Pessoa, Sá-Carneiro had a horror of madness and abnormality in general, the reason, perhaps, why the whole of his work was a concerted effort to exorcise those demons.

Whatever the truth of that, *Lúcio's Confession*, with its irresistible and unbearably intense mixture of innovation and convention, of aberrance and beauty, of death and love, of madness and lucidity, will stand as one of the most interesting and revealing documents left by the argonauts of that great Portuguese adventure, Primeiro Modernismo.

Eugénio Lisboa

After spending ten years in prison for a crime I did not commit but against which I offered no defence, numb now to life and to dreams, with nothing more to hope for and no desires, I have finally come to make my confession, that is, to prove my innocence.

You may not believe me, indeed I am sure you will not. But that is of little consequence. I have absolutely no interest now in telling the world that I did not murder Ricardo de Loureiro. I have no family; I have no need of vindication. Besides, the simple truth is that there can be no vindication for someone who has spent the last ten years in prison.

And to those who ask, having read what I have written: 'But why did you not speak out at the time? Why did you not prove your innocence at the trial?' to them I will reply: My defence was untenable. No one would have believed me. And what point was there in being taken for a liar or a madman? I should explain too that I was left so shattered by the events in which I found myself caught up, that the prospect of prison seemed to me almost a pleasant one. It meant oblivion, tranquillity, sleep. It simply provided an ending, a conclusion to my devastated life. All I wanted then was for the trial to be over and for my sentence to begin.

For the rest, the trial passed swiftly. Well, it seemed like an open-and-shut case. I neither denied anything nor confessed. But silence gives consent. Besides, everyone felt a certain sympathy for me.

The crime was, as the newspapers of the time no doubt put it, a 'crime of passion', a case of *Cherchez la femme*. What's more the victim was a poet, an artist. The woman involved had made herself a still more romantic figure by vanishing. I was, in short, a hero, a hero with a hint of mystery about me, which only added to my glamour. For all these reasons, not to mention the splendid speech made by the defence, the jury concluded that there were extenuating circumstances and my sentence was therefore a short one.

Ah, how short a time it was – especially for me. Those ten years flew by as if they had been ten months. For time means nothing to someone who has felt his whole life condensed into a single moment. When you have endured the worst suffering, nothing can ever make you suffer again. When you have known the most intense of feelings, nothing can ever move you again. The fact is that very few people have experienced such a culminating moment. Those who have either do as I did and join the ranks of the living dead or else become one of the disenchanted who all too often end by taking their own lives.

I cannot honestly say that the greater happiness is *not* to experience such a moment. Those who do not may at least enjoy peace of mind. But the truth is that everyone hopes for such a moment of enlightenment. Therefore, no one is happy, which is why, despite everything, I am proud to have done so.

But enough of these speculations. I am not writing a novel. I simply wish to provide a clear exposition of the facts. And it seems to me that, if my aim is clarity, then I am setting off along the wrong road. Besides, however lucid I may intend to be, my confession will – of this I am sure – seem utterly incoherent, disturbing and very far from lucid.

One thing I can guarantee though, I will not omit a single detail, however small or apparently inconsequential. In cases such as the one I am attempting to explain, enlightenment can only grow out of a great number of facts, and facts are all I will give. People may draw what conclusions they like from these facts. For my part, I have never tried to do so. If I did, I would surely go mad.

What I will say again, on my word of honour, is that what I set down here is the truth. Whether or not you believe me is unimportant. However unbelievable it may seem, what I am about to tell you *is* the absolute truth.

My confession is merely a statement of fact.

I

Around 1895, how I don't quite know, I found myself studying Law – or rather not studying Law – at the University of Paris. I had been something of a drifter since adolescence and, having tried out various 'goals' in life, only to abandon each in turn, I was gripped by a desire to see Europe and I decided to take myself off to its capital, Paris. I soon became embroiled in various vaguely artistic circles and Gervásio Vila-Nova, whom I had known slightly in Lisbon, became my constant companion. He cut a curious figure, that of the great artist *manqué*, or rather, of the artist doomed to failure.

There was something disquieting about his tall, gaunt, angular body, with its dual and contradictory suggestion of both a hysterical, narcotic effeminacy and a sallow asceticism. When his long hair fell back from his face to reveal a broad, firm but terribly pale brow, it evoked images of hairshirts and extreme abstinence; yet when it fell forward in waves over his forehead, it evoked only tenderness, the troubling tenderness of golden ecstasies and subtle kisses. He always dressed in black, in long jackets that had a touch of the priest about them, an impression reinforced by the type of collar he wore, narrow and close-fitting. When his forehead was concealed by his hair or by a hat, there was nothing enigmatic about his face at all, quite the contrary. Oddly enough though, there *was* something mysterious about his body, something that made one think of sphinxes, perhaps, on moonlit nights. It was not his actual physiognomy that etched itself upon one's memory, but rather his strange personality. He stood out in every crowd, he was stared at, talked about, although, in fact, at first sight there seemed to be nothing very remarkable about his appearance: his clothes, albeit of a slightly exaggerated cut, were black, his hair, though long, was never extravagantly so, and his hat, a woollen beret, whilst certainly odd, was no different from that worn by many artists.

The truth is that Gervásio Vila-Nova had an aura about him. He was the sort of man you look at in the street and say: he must be someone important.

Women utterly adored him. They would watch in fascination whenever he wandered, tall and arrogant, into a café . . . But they looked at him more the way women look at some exquisitely beautiful and bejewelled member of their own sex.

'You know, my dear Lúcio,' he often said to me, 'I never possess my lovers, they possess me.'

When we talked, his flame burned even brighter. He was a brilliant conversationalist, lovable despite his many solecisms, despite his mistakes (which he would defend passionately and always successfully), despite his repellent but nonetheless glorious opinions, despite his paradoxes, his lies. He was a superior being, there was no doubt about it, one of those people who remains engraved on our memory, who troubles and obsesses us. He was fire, pure fire!

However, if you examined him with your intelligence, rather than with your emotions, you would see at once that there was, alas, nothing beyond the aura, that his genius – perhaps too brilliant – would consume itself, remain unsublimated into work and end up dispersed, fragmented, burned out. And that, in fact, is exactly what happened. He avoided failure only because he had the courage to destroy himself first.

It was impossible to feel affection for someone like that (although deep down he was an excellent fellow), and yet even today I recall with nostalgia the talks we had, the nights spent in cafés and I can even convince myself that, yes, the fate of Gervásio Vila-Nova really was the most beautiful of fates and that he was a great artist, an artist of genius.

My friend had many contacts in the artistic world: writers, painters and musicians from every country. One morning, he came into my room and announced:

'Yesterday, my dear Lúcio, I was introduced to a most

interesting American woman. She's fabulously rich and lives in a mansion she's had specially built – on Avenue du Bois de Boulogne, if you please – on a site previously occupied by two large buildings which she simply ordered to be demolished. She's an enchanting woman. The man who introduced her to me was that American painter with the blue-tinted spectacles. Do you know who I mean? I can't remember his name ... Anyway she can be found every afternoon in the Pavillon d'Armenonville. She takes tea there. I'd like you to meet her. You'll see what I mean then. A fascinating woman!'

The following day turned out warm and sunny – one of those splendid winter afternoons of blue skies – and we hired a carriage and set off for that celebrated restaurant. Once there, we sat down and ordered tea. Barely ten minutes had passed when Gervásio touched my arm. A group of eight people were coming into the salon – three women and five men. Of the women, two were blonde and petite with skin the colour of roses and milk and bodies that were both sensual and well-proportioned – identical, in fact, to so many other adorable English girls. But the third woman had a beauty that was redolent of mystery and dreams. She was tall and thin with a long face and golden skin and extraordinary hair of a startling fiery red. Hers was a beauty that inspired awe. In fact, the moment I saw her, my feeling was one of fear, the sort of fear you might experience when coming face to face with someone you know to have committed some vile and monstrous deed.

She sat down silently but, the moment she saw us, came running over to Gervásio with her arms outstretched:

'My dear, how delightful to see you ... Why only yesterday, someone was singing your praises to me ... A fellow countryman of yours ... a poet ... a M. de Loureiro, I think.'

The Portuguese name was rendered almost unintelligible by her garbled pronunciation.

'Oh, I didn't know he was in Paris,' murmured Gervásio.

And to me, once he had made the proper introductions, he said:

'Do you know him? The poet, Ricardo de Loureiro, he wrote *Embers* . . .'

I said that I had never spoken to him, but knew him by sight and admired his work intensely.

'Indeed . . . I won't argue with you there . . . but, as you know, I find that kind of art distinctly *passé*. It holds no interest for me . . . Give me the *sauvages* any time!'

This was one of Gervásio Vila-Nova's many affectations: heaping praise on the latest pseudo-literary movement, in this case, *sauvagisme*, whose one novelty lay in the fact that its proponents' books were printed on various types of paper, in different-coloured inks, and arranged eccentrically on the page in extravagant typefaces. They, the poets and prosewriters of the *sauvagiste* movement, had also – and this is what most thrilled my friend – abolished 'that vile thing' the idea, and they expressed their emotions purely through the use of syllabic games and strange, outlandish onomatopoeia. They even created new, entirely meaningless words, whose beauty, according to them, lay precisely in their lack of meaning. It seems that only one book had actually been published by this school, by some Russian poet with an unpronounceable name, a book Gervásio had certainly never read, but whose virtues he nonetheless never tired of extolling, declaring it to be astonishing, a work of genius.

The foreign woman invited us to join her at her table and introduced us to her male companions, whom we had not met before: the journalist, Jean Lamy, from *Le Figaro*, the Dutch painter, Van Derk, and the English sculptor, Thomas Westwood. The two other men present were the American painter with the blue-tinted spectacles and the small, perplexing figure of the Vicomte de Naudières, blond, diaphanous and heavily made-up. As for the two girls, she merely pointed to them and said:

'Jenny and Dora.'

The conversation immediately became ultra-civilised and

banal. We talked about fashion, discussed the theatre and the music hall, with a great deal of chat about art thrown in. And the person who most distinguished himself, indeed almost monopolised the talk, was Gervásio. As happened to everyone when they were with him, we were all overwhelmed by his intensity and reduced either to listening or, at most, protesting, that is, to giving him every opportunity to shine.

'You know, my dear Lúcio,' he said to me once, 'Fonseca says that going around with me is an art in itself. A difficult, exhausting art. It's because I'm always talking. I never allow my companion to rest. I oblige him to be intense, to react. And, I agree, you're absolutely right, my company can be tiring.'

'You' – let it be said – denoted everyone except Gervásio. And Fonseca, for his part, was a poor little painter from Madeira, 'an ex-public servant' with a scrubby beard, who wore *lavalière* cravats and smoked a pipe. He was a silent, vapid fellow, always staring nostalgically into space, longing perhaps for his lost island . . . A sweet boy!

After much talk about the theatre and after Gervásio had proclaimed that actors – even the greatest, like Bernhardt or Novelli – were never more than mummers, mere intellectuals who *learned* their parts, and after he had assured us – 'believe me, my friends, I'm right about this' – that true art existed only amongst acrobats (these acrobats were one of his hobbyhorses and the very first night we met in Paris, he had told me, in confidence, a macabre tale of being kidnapped by a company of jugglers when he was only two years old, his parents having despatched him, in a display of barbarous cruelty, to a wetnurse from the Serra da Estrela, the wife of a potter, from whom he had doubtless inherited his talent for sculpture and of whom, in fact, due to a mix-up over cradles, he was possibly even the son), the conversation somehow turned to the subject of sensuality in art.

At this point the strange American woman immediately protested:

'I really don't think you should be discussing the role of sensuality in art, for, my friends, sensuality *is* an art, possibly the most beautiful of all the arts. Up until now, however, very few have cultivated it in that spirit. Imagine trembling with waves of incipient pleasure, with ecstasies of fire, aflame with longing – wouldn't that be a pleasure to thrill you, so much more intense than the vague frisson of beauty a superb painting or a poem in bronze might afford you? Believe me it would. Of course, you would need to know how to kindle those waves of pleasure, *how to provoke them*. And that is precisely what no one knows, what no one even considers. So the pleasures of the senses are the same for everyone, they are purely carnal pleasures, mere brute embraces, wet kisses, repellently moist caresses. Ah, but what wonderful, extraordinary works could be created by a truly great artist, who took sensuality as his raw material. At his disposal he would have fire, light, air, water, sound, colour, smells, opiates and silks – all those new and as yet unexplored sensual experiences . . . I would be proud to be that artist! My dream is to hold a great party in my enchanted palace, where I would overwhelm you all with pleasure . . . where I would rain down on you the tremulous mysteries of light, of many-coloured fires, so that for the first time your flesh would really feel the fire and the light, the perfumes and the sounds, which, penetrating it, would be scattered, dissolved, destroyed! . . . Have you never considered the strange voluptuousness of fire, the perversity of water, the sensual subtleties of light? Whenever I plunge my bare legs into the waters of a stream, whenever I gaze upon the incandescent flames of a fire or feel my body lit by electric torrents of light, I must confess I feel real sexual excitement – an excitement in which desire has been ennobled by beauty. Believe me, my friends, however refined, however complicated and however much the artist you all pretend to be, you are, in fact, mere barbarians!'

Gervásio rebelled against this. Sensuality was not an art. Asceticism and self-denial, yes, but sensuality raised to the level of an art form? A banal idea . . . It was what everyone said or, deep down, thought.

And he continued in that vein, arguing against the idea, letting it be known in the most charming way possible that he did so purely because he believed it to be such a commonplace.

Throughout the conversation, the only people not to utter a word were the two English girls, Jenny and Dora, who, however, never once took their pale blue eyes off Gervásio.

Everyone had changed places by then and Gervásio was sitting next to the American woman. They made a very handsome couple. Their profiles matched each other perfectly, sculpted by the same shadows – two wild beasts of love, singular, disquieting, morbidly evocative of enigmatic perfumes, yellow moons, purple twilights, of beauty, perversity, vice, disease . . .

But night had fallen. A pair of lovers from the *beau monde* entered to find shelter in that famous establishment, almost deserted in winter.

The eccentric American woman gave the signal to leave and when she stood up, I noticed, with some trepidation, that she was wearing strange sandals on her bare feet . . . and that her toenails were painted gold.

At the Porte Maillot, we took the tram to Montparnasse and Gervásio said:

'So, Lúcio, what did you think of my American?'

'Very interesting.'

'Really? But you probably don't like that sort of person. I quite understand. Yours is a simple nature, and so . . .'

'On the contrary,' I said, in idiotic protest, 'I greatly admire such people. I find them extremely interesting. And as for my simple nature . . .'

'I admit that, for my part, I adore such creatures . . . I feel immense tenderness for them, an extraordinary affinity . . . as I do for pederasts . . . for prostitutes . . . Oh, it's terrible, my friend, terrible . . .'

I merely smiled. I was used to this. I knew perfectly well that it all boiled down to one thing only: *Art*.

For Gervásio started from the principle that the artist does not reveal himself in his works, rather, indeed uniquely, in his personality. This meant that, for him, the work of an artist was basically of little importance. He required, however, that an artist be interesting and brilliant in his physical appearance, in his behaviour – in short, in his external way of being.

'Because, my friend, giving the name of artist and man of genius to a ridiculous, fat old man like Balzac, hunched and odious, who is vulgar in his conversation and in his views, is simply wrong, it is neither fair nor permissible.'

'But what about . . . ,' I would protest, citing truly great artists, all of unprepossessing physical appearance.

And Gervásio Vila-Nova would always be ready with an unanswerable reply.

If, for example – though this rarely happened – the name mentioned was that of an artist whose work he himself had once praised, he would say:

'Forgive me, my friend, but you're really not being very perceptive. The man of whom you speak, although apparently mediocre, is a man of great passion. Surely you know that he . . .'

And then he would invent some interesting anecdote, beautiful and intense, to attribute to his man . . .

And I would say nothing.

Besides, that was another habit of Gervásio's: making people what he wanted them to be, not seeing them as they really were. If he was introduced to someone with whom, for whatever reason, he felt in sympathy, he would immediately attribute to him or her the kind of opinions and manners that he liked, even though, in fact, the person was the antithesis of all that. Obviously a day would come when disillusion would set in, but he was capable of maintaining the illusion for some considerable time . . .

On the way home that night, I could not refrain from remarking to him:

'Did you notice, her feet were bare and she was wearing sandals . . . and her toenails were painted gold.'

'Are you sure? I don't believe it . . .'

That strange woman had made a powerful impression on me and, before going to sleep, I thought about her and her group of friends for a long time.

Ah, but Gervásio was right. Deep down, I did hate those people – *the artists.* That is, those false artists whose work consists of the poses they strike: saying outrageous things, cultivating complicated tastes and appetites, being artificial, irritating, unbearable. People who, in fact, take from art only what is false and external.

But then, another idea would surface in my confused spirit: if I hated them, it was probably only because I envied them and could not be like them.

Whatever the truth of the matter, even if I really did hate them, the fact is that I still felt drawn to them as if by some pernicious vice.

I didn't see Gervásio for a whole week after that, something which happened only rarely.

At the end of that week, he came to see me and said:

'I've been getting to know our American friend better. She really is a most intriguing creature and terribly artistic. Those two little English girls are her lovers. She's a follower of Sappho.'

'Surely not . . .'

'She is.'

And we said no more about her.

A month went by. I had already forgotten all about the flame-haired woman, when one night, Gervásio suddenly announced to me:

'By the way, that American woman I introduced to you the other day is giving a big party tomorrow and you're invited.'

'Me?'

'Yes. She told me to bring some friends and she mentioned you. She likes you a lot. It should be interesting. There's a performance at the end – apotheosis and dance or something . . . If you don't want to come, don't. I know how that sort of thing bores you . . .'

As usual, I protested, like the idiot I still was, and declared that, on the contrary, I had every intention of going with him, and we arranged to meet the following night at ten in the Closerie.

On the day of the party, I regretted having agreed to go. I felt such an aversion to society life . . . Quite apart from having to put on a dinner jacket and waste a whole evening . . . Oh well . . .

When I reached the café, I found, much to my surprise, that my friend had already arrived. He said to me:

'We still have to wait for Ricardo de Loureiro. He's invited too. And I arranged to meet him here. Look, there he is.'

And he introduced us:

'The writer Lúcio Vaz . . . the poet Ricardo de Loureiro.'

And we, in turn, said to one another:

'Delighted to meet you.'

Along the way we struck up conversation and, from the very first, I took a great liking to Ricardo de Loureiro. His Arab-dark face, with its strong lines, revealed a frank, open nature, illumined by intense, dark brown eyes, bright with intelligence.

I spoke to him about his work, which I admired, and he told me that he had read my volume of short stories and had been especially intrigued by a story called *João Tortura*. Whilst I found this opinion flattering, it also made me feel even more warmly towards the poet, perceiving in him a nature that might understand my own soul a little. For that story was far and away my own particular favourite, but it was the only one that no critic had ever mentioned, and one that even my friends, without actually saying so, believed to be my least successful.

The artist's conversation was both brilliant and captivating and, for the first time, I saw Gervásio, who normally dominated every group he was in, fall silent and listen.

At last our coupé pulled up outside a magnificent mansion on the Avenue du Bois de Boulogne. It was fantastically lit from within by a blaze of light filtered through red silk curtains. A large number of carriages stood at the door, an odd mixture of shabby fiacres and a few splendid private carriages.

We got out.

At the entrance, a servant took our invitations from us, as if we were in a theatre foyer, whilst another immediately ushered us over to a lift that whisked us up to the first floor. There an astonishing sight awaited us: a large elliptical room, the ceiling of which was a lofty, glittering cupola supported on multi-coloured columns crowned by splendid volutes. At the far end of this room, resting upon bronze sphinxes, stood a strange stage from which – down a flight of pink marble steps – you descended into a large semi-circular swimming pool full of translucent water. There were also three tiers of galleries, so that the whole room looked exactly like some fantastic, sumptuous theatre.

Somewhere a hidden orchestra was grinding out waltzes.

When we went in – inevitably – every eye fixed on Gervásio Vila-Nova, looking priestly and exceptionally handsome in his black waisted jacket. The American woman immediately rushed up to us to ask what we thought of the room. The architects had only put the finishing touches to it two weeks before. This lavish party was being held to celebrate its inauguration.

We all gave loud expression to our astonishment at the marvellous room and she, the enchantress, smiled mysteriously and said: 'I want to know your opinion about what happens later on . . . *especially the lights*.'

The American woman was wearing an extraordinary dress, a kind of tunic made from a most singular material, impossible to describe. It was like a closely woven mesh of metallic threads – made from the most diverse metals – that fused together to produce an appearance of shimmering fire, a fire that contained all the colours in the world alternately colliding in shrill harmony or merging to produce whistling, starry tumults of reflected light. *Her tunic was colour gone mad.*

If you looked closely you could see her bare skin through the mesh of the fabric. The nipple of one breast poked through, firm and golden.

Her red hair was arranged in disorderly coils threaded with precious stones, which clustered like stars amidst flames, throwing off rays of transcendent light. Emerald serpents curled and bit about her arms but she wore not a single jewel upon her deep décolletage. She was like a disquieting statue to serpentine desire, to platinum depravity. And what emanated from her skin, in that blue penumbra, was the dense aroma of transgression.

After a few moments, she slipped quickly away to greet other guests.

The room had filled up meanwhile with a strange and extravagant multitude. There were foreign women in daring ball gowns that left them almost naked and men with suspicious-looking faces above the unisonous black of male evening dress. There were red-haired, hirsute Russians, palely blond Scandinavians, stocky, curly-haired southerners, a Chinese man and an Indian. It was the quintessence of cosmopolitan Paris – brilliant, opulent and gaudy.

The guests danced and talked until midnight. Up in the galleries people gambled furiously. But then supper was announced and we all went into the dining room, which furnished us with yet further marvels.

Shortly before, the American woman had come over to us and whispered confidentially:

'After supper comes the show – my Triumph! I've tried to summarise in it all my ideas about sensuality as an art. Lights, bodies, smells, fire and water – everything will come together in an orgy of flesh distilled into gold!'

... ...

When we came back into the large salon, I, for my part, felt afraid and shrank back.

The whole scene had changed, it felt like a completely different room. It was filled by a heavy perfume, tremulous with passion. A mysterious breeze blew through it, *a grey breeze blotched with yellow* – I don't know why but that, for some strange reason, is how it seemed to me, a breeze that made our skin prick and shiver. The most astonishing and remarkable thing, however, was the lighting. I feel quite incapable of describing it. I could only, with great effort, attempt to explain its singularity, its languorous power.

The light – electric light of course – came from an infinite number of strange, round glass lampshades in a variety of colours and designs and of varying degrees of transparency, but in particular from the waves of brilliant light that blazed forth from projectors concealed in the galleries. Now these torrents of light, all focused on the same chimerical point in space, came together to form a maelstrom, and it was out of that meteoric maelstrom that the beams of light, ricocheting one against the other, were projected back onto walls and columns, were scattered about the room, transforming it.

The light in the room was, in effect, a projection of itself, it was still light, of course, but the truth is that the marvellous thing illuminating us did not seem like light. It seemed like something else, some sort of new fluid. I'm not talking nonsense here, I'm simply describing a real sensation, for we did not so much see that light as feel it. And I don't think it would be going too far to say that it did not so much affect our sight as our sense of touch. *If our eyes had been suddenly torn from us, we would still have been able to see it*. What's more – and this is the most bizarre and splendid part – we could breathe this strange fluid. It's true, we drank in that light together with the air, with the purple perfume of the air, a light which, in a moment of iridescent ecstasy, of dizzying elation, flooded our lungs, invaded our blood, suffused our bodies with sound. Yes, that magical light actually resonated inside us, enlarging our senses, filling us with harmonies, flowing through us, dazzling us . . . Under its influence, our flesh became open to every sensation, every smell, every melody!

And we, our senses honed by long exposure to culture and art, were not alone in feeling overwhelmed by that shimmering mystery. For it was soon clear from the confused faces and troubled gestures of everyone in the audience that, engulfed by that light from beyond Hell, by that *sexualised* light, they were all transfixed as if under the spell of some flame-red sorcery.

But suddenly the light changed, became an arcing fall, and another tremor ran through us, milder this time, like a flurry of emerald kisses after a series of bruising bites.

In this new dawn, a vibrant music jingled forth in strange rhythms – a slender melody in which clashing segments of crystal lay submerged, in which sword-sharp palm leaves cooled the air, in which moist sequences of subtle sounds evaporated . . .

In short, we were all on the point of swooning in one final spasm of the soul . . . but they had sustained us this long only in order to prolong our pleasure.

At the far end of the room, the curtain rose on an aurora stage. The light that had so troubled us was extinguished and we were lit only by torrents of white electricity.

Three dancers appeared on the stage. They wore their hair loose and their upper bodies were clothed in tight scarlet blouses that left their breasts tremulously free. Tenuous strips of gauze hung from their waists. There was a gap between blouse and gauze – a stripe of bare flesh on which symbolic flowers were painted.

The dancers began their dance. Their legs were bare. They span, jumped, then merged into one, entangling limbs, kissing one another hard on the mouth.

The first dancer had black hair, her skin was resplendent as the sun. Her legs, seemingly moulded out of golden dawn, stole forth into the radiant light, to reveal, near her pubis, a mordant flesh one longed to sink one's teeth into.

But what made the dancers so exciting was the limpid nostalgia they evoked for a great blue lake of crystalline water where, on moonlit nights, they would plunge in, barefoot and tender.

The second dancer had the look of a perverse adolescent. She was thin, though with quite developed breasts, and had dull blonde hair, a provocative face and a turned-up nose. Her legs, knotted with muscles, were hard, masculine and aroused in everyone present the violent urge to bite them.

The third and final dancer was the most disquieting. She was ice-cool and slender, very pale and gaunt, her skeletal, devastated legs evocative of mysticism and disease.

Meanwhile, the dance continued. Their movements grew gradually faster and faster until, at last, in one final spasm, their mouths met and, with all the veils torn away – breasts, bellies, vulvas all uncovered – their bodies lay entangled, dying in a frenzy of desire.

And the curtain fell returning us to that earlier luminous placidity . . .

Other admirable scenes followed: naked dancers chasing each other in the pool, mimicking the sexual nature of the water, strange dancers scattering perfumes that lent an eerie darkness to the already fantastical atmosphere of the room; apotheoses of bare bodies piled one upon the other – sensual visions of vivid colour, vortices of ecstasy, symphonies of silks and velvets whirling about naked flesh.

But, however perverse, none of these marvels aroused in us lubricious or bestial desires, rather they stirred up an extraordinary and delicious longing in the soul that both burned and soothed.

An impression of excess passed only fleetingly through us.

But it was not only the lewd scenes that provoked the ecstasies stirring in our souls. Far from it. What we experienced created in us an all-embracing sensation identical to what one would feel when listening to a sublime suite performed by an orchestra of virtuosi. And the sensual tableaux were simply one instrument in that orchestra, the other instruments being the lights, the perfumes, the colours . . . Yes, all those elements fused into an admirable whole which, by expanding the soul, penetrated it, and which our souls perceived as a distant fever, a vibration in the depths. We were all soul. *Even our carnal desires descended to us from our souls.*

However, this was as nothing compared to the final vision.

The lights became denser, sharper and more penetrating, falling now in torrents from the apex of the cupola and the curtain drew back to reveal a vaguely Asiatic scene . . . To the sound of heavy, hoarse, distant music, *she* appeared, the woman with red hair.

And she began to dance.

She was wrapped in a white tunic striped with yellow. Her hair hung down, wild and loose. She wore fantastic jewels on her fingers and her bare feet glittered with precious stones.

How to describe her silent steps, wet and cold as crystal; the stormy surges of her undulating body; the alcohol of her lips which – a brilliant touch this – she had painted gold; the evanescent harmony of her gestures; the whole diffuse horizon tenuously evoked by her whirling figure?

Meanwhile, on a mysterious altar behind her, fire burst forth.

In slow degrees of abandonment her tunic slipped from her body until, in a spasm of restrained ecstasy, it fell at her feet. Ah, at that point, confronted by the marvellous sight transfixing us, we could not help but cry out in amazement.

Chimerical, naked, her rarefied body rose up solemnly amidst a thousand fantastic coruscations. Like her lips, her nipples and her vulva were painted gold – a pale, sickly gold. And, in her desire to give herself to the fire, her whole being swayed in the grip of a scarlet mysticism.

But the fire drove her back.

Then, in a final act of perversity, she put on her veils again and hid herself, leaving only her golden vulva uncovered – a terrible flower of flesh moving in convulsive magenta spasms.

She was all victorious, all fire.

Then, naked again, fiery and fierce, she jumped into the flames, tearing at them, ensnaring and *possessing* them as they twined drunkenly about her.

But, at last, exhausted after all these strange convulsions, she landed, in one prodigious leap, like a meteor – a flame-haired meteor – in the lake that a thousand hidden lights painted an ashy blue.

Then came the apotheosis.

As the blue water received her body, it grew red as burning coals, troubled and burned by her flesh which the fire had penetrated . . . And in her desire to extinguish that fire, the naked, possessed creature plunged in, but the deeper in she went, the brighter the light about her.

Until at last, mysteriously, the fire faded into gold and her dead body floated, heraldic, upon the gilded waters – now calm and dead as well.

... ...

Normal light filled the room again. Only just in time. Women flailed about in the grip of hysteria; men with flushed faces made incoherent gestures.

The doors opened and we, lost and hatless, found ourselves once more out in the street, aflame, perplexed. The cool night air beat about us, forcing us awake, as if we had just returned from a dream all three of us had dreamed. Dumbstruck, we looked at each other with troubled eyes . . .

The marvels we had seen had made such a powerful impression on us that we hadn't the strength to say a word.

Crushed, stunned, we went our separate ways home.

The following evening, after sleeping for eleven hours, I found it impossible to believe in the existence of that strange orgy: The Orgy of Fire, as Ricardo later called it.

I went out. I dined.

When I entered the Café Riche, someone tapped me on the shoulder:

'How are you, my friend? Tell me, what did you think of it?'

It was Ricardo de Loureiro.

We talked for a long time about the extraordinary things we had witnessed. And the poet said that it seemed more like the vision of some brilliant onanist than mere reality.

As for the American woman with the red hair, I never saw her again. Even Gervásio never mentioned her. And, as if it were a mystery from the Beyond to which we judged it best not to allude, we never again spoke of that remarkable night.

If the memory of it has remained forever engraved on my mind, it is not because I happened to experience it, but because my friendship with Ricardo de Loureiro dates from that night.

For that is how things are. We connect certain events in our lives to other more fundamental ones and, often, a whole world, a whole humanity, can centre on one simple kiss.

Besides, in the present case, what importance could one

fantastic night have in comparison with our meeting, *the meeting that marked the beginning of my life?*

Any friendship that had its beginnings against such a strange, disquieting, golden backdrop must have been fore-ordained by fate . . .

II

Within a month, Ricardo and I had become not merely inseparable companions but close and sincere friends, between whom there were no misunderstandings nor even secrets.

My association with Gervásio Vila-Nova had ceased completely. In fact, he returned to Portugal shortly afterwards.

Ah, how different this new friendship was, how much more spontaneous, affectionate! And how different we were from Gervásio Vila-Nova who, apropos of almost anything, would make statements such as:

'You know, Lúcio, you can't imagine how it hurts me that people don't like my work.' (His 'work' consisted of figures without heads or feet, for he sculpted only torsos, contorted, intertwined, monstrous torsos, certain details of which, however, revealed a skilled chisel at work.) 'But don't go thinking it's myself I feel sorry for. I know my work is good. I feel sorry for *them*, poor things, because they can't see its beauty.'

Or else:

'Believe me, my friend, it really isn't a good idea to work for those cheap magazines back home . . . to be in such a hurry to get your books published. The true artist should keep his work unpublished for as long as possible. For example, have you ever known me to have an exhibition? The only way to publish a book is in a limited edition at 100 francs a copy, as did . . .' (and he would cite the Russian leader of the *sauvagistes*). 'I abhore publicity!'

My conversations with Ricardo – an interesting point this – were, from the start, conversations from the soul rather than the usual conversations intellectuals have.

For the first time, in fact, I had met someone capable of descending, even if only a little way, into the unvisited recesses of my spirit, which for me were also the most sensitive and painful. And, as he told me later, he felt the same.

Not that we were happy, oh no! Our lives were tormented by desires, misunderstandings, obscure sufferings.

We had risen to a higher plane, we hovered above life. We could have grown drunk on pride, had we wanted to – but we suffered so much, so very much. Our one refuge was our work.

In describing his anxieties, Ricardo de Loureiro made disturbing confessions to me, employed strange images:

'Ah, my dear Lúcio, believe me, nothing pleases me any more, everything bores me, sickens me. My few enthusiasms, should I think of them, soon evaporate, for when I weigh them up, I find them to be so mean, so shoddy . . . Shall I tell you something? At night in bed, before going to sleep, I used to allow myself to daydream. And, for brief moments, I would be happy, lost in imaginings of glory, love, ecstasy . . . But I no longer know what dreams I could use to fortify myself. I've already built all my castles in Spain . . . and grown tired of them: they're always the same and besides there are no more to be found now . . . Anyway, it isn't just the things I already have that bore me, I hate the things I don't have as well, because, in life as in dreams, they're always the same. Moreover, if I occasionally suffer because I don't possess certain things that have not, as yet, become all too familiar, the truth is that, when I look deeper into myself, I immediately see that, my God, if I had them, my pain, my tedium would be even greater . . . So *wasting* time is now the one aim of my empty life. If I travel, if I write, if, in short, I live, believe me, I do so only in order to use up the minutes. But soon – I can feel it happening already – this too will bore me. And then what will I do? I don't know, I really don't . . . everything seems so infinitely bitter.'

I would try to cheer him up, would tell him abjectly that he must put aside such depressing ideas. A splendid future lay before him. He must take courage!

'A splendid future? Look, my friend, up until now I've

never even been able to see myself in the future at all. And the things I can't see, never happen.'

This answer left me dumbstruck and I could only look at him questioningly. Ricardo said:

'Ah, of course, perhaps you don't understand . . . I've never explained that to you. Listen, it's something I've done ever since I was a child . . . When I think about possible situations in my life, I look ahead and I either see myself in them or I don't. For example, one place where I've never been able to see myself is in life itself – anyway could you really say that what we have is a life? But let me explain more clearly . . . in my childish imagination I used to dream, to create a thousand wonderful, heroic adventures, the way all children do. Well, when I imagined them, I never saw myself as actually experiencing them later on. And to date, I am the only person who has never appeared in a single one of those delightful episodes. Not because I ran away from them. I've never run away from anything.

A rather odd, even somewhat awkward situation arose in my life at one point. I would often tell myself that this sad affair would have to come to an end. And I knew of a very natural ending. However, I never imagined myself being part of that ending. I imagined some other ending. That other ending, however, could only take place with my intervention. And, this much was clear, that was the one way it could not, indeed should not, take place. Time passed. I need hardly say that it was precisely that impossibility that came to be.

Although I was a good student, I never envisaged myself finishing my course. And one fine day, quite suddenly and for no apparent reason, I left university and fled to Paris.

I never imagined myself participating in everyday life either. So far, and I'm twenty-seven now, I have still never managed to earn a living from my work. Luckily, I don't need to. And I've never really managed to enter into life, into ordinary Life with a capital L – social life, if you like. It's odd, I'm an outsider who knows half of Paris, an outcast with no debts and not a stain on my character, whom everyone respects, and who, nevertheless, belongs nowhere. It's true. In fact, I never *saw* myself as belonging anywhere. Even in the circles I've become involved with, I don't know why, but I've always felt a stranger.

And it's terrible; it torments me sometimes this gift of mine. So much so that if I can't physically *see* a particular project that I feel keen to undertake, then there is no way I can carry it out and I quickly become disenchanted with the idea, even if, deep down, I consider it an admirable one.

To put it still more clearly, this feeling is similar, albeit in reverse, to another of which you've probably heard – which you may even have experienced – that of *déjà vu*. Has it never happened to you that you visit a country or a place for the first time and – like a distant recollection, vague and troubling – you are assailed by the thought that – *where or when you don't know* – you have already been in that country, gazed on that scene?

You may not understand what these two ideas have in common. I'm not sure I can explain, but I sense, indeed I'm sure, that there *is* a connection.'

I mumbled a reply and the poet added:

'But I haven't told you the strangest part yet. Do you know, I cannot imagine myself growing old, just as I cannot imagine myself ill or dying. Nor even killing myself, as I've tried at times to fool myself I would. And so great is my confidence in this superstition that, were I not absolutely sure that we all must die, I swear I would not believe in my own death, because I cannot *see* myself dead.'

I smiled at this *boutade*.

Some vague acquaintances came into the café where we were sitting. They joined us and, with banal facility, the conversation glided onto another plane.

Ricardo came up with equally bizarre revelations on other occasions too, revelations slightly reminiscent of Vila-

Nova's pretentious utterances. But I knew that everything Ricardo said was true and deeply felt. At least, deeply felt in the same way literature is deeply felt. As Ricardo explained to me one night:

'I guarantee you, my friend, that all the ideas that appear in my work, however strange, however impossible, are all, at least in part, genuine. That is, they translate emotions I have really felt, ideas I've actually had about certain aspects of my own psychology. All that happens is that they sometimes arrive in the world already fictionalised.'

But to return to his bizarre revelations . . .

We often took the opportunity to plunge back into normal life and forget about ourselves, frequenting theatres and music halls out of a desire to feel part of such intensely contemporary places, so European, so glamorous.

Thus, one night in the Olympia, we were watching some English dancers who were appearing in a review there, when Ricardo asked me:

'Tell me, Lúcio, are you never prey to sudden mad, inexplicable fears?'

Not really, I replied, at least only very vaguely.

'Well,' he said, 'I am. Do you want to know something? I'm afraid of those dancers.'

I laughed out loud at this but Ricardo continued:

'The reason is, I don't know if you've noticed it, but now all the fashionable music halls put on these dances performed by troupes of English girls. The creatures are all the same, always, they wear the same costumes, have the same bare legs, the same unremarkable features, the same charming air about them. So there is no way I can make myself think of them as individuals. I can't imagine them having a life – a lover, a past, particular habits, certain personality traits. I can't disentangle them from the whole group, that's what frightens me. I'm not putting this on, my friend, really I'm not.

But not all my fears are like that. I have many others. For example, I have a horror of arches, of certain triumphal arches but, in particular, of some of the old arches you find in ordinary streets. It's not really the arches themselves I'm afraid of, it's the empty space that they provide a frame for. I still remember the mysterious feeling of terror I had when I discovered at the end of a solitary road in some capital city or other, a small arch, or rather a door, open onto the infinite. For that's exactly what it was. In fact the road was an incline and the monument doubtless stood at the top of that incline, so that, from a distance, you could only see sky through that arch. I confess that I stood for a good few minutes just staring at it, fascinated. I was seized by a strong desire to continue on up to the end of the road to see where it led. But my courage failed me. I fled, terrified. And that feeling was so strong that now I can't even remember in which sad city I felt it.

When I was young, I used to be, and indeed still am, terrified of Gothic arches in cathedrals, of vaults, of the shadows cast by tall columns, of obelisks and sweeping marble staircases. My whole psychological life has been a projection of those childhood thoughts, amplified and modified, but still following the same course, the same order; they just operate on a different level now.

And, lastly, still on the subject of phobias, just as I'm frightened of empty spaces framed by arches, something else that troubles me is the sky above certain streets, those narrow streets lined with tall buildings that suddenly open up to reveal tight arcs of sky.'

He was certainly in the mood for the bizarre that night, for he made further odd remarks to me as we left the theatre.

'You'll be amazed to hear this, my dear Lúcio, but I can guarantee you that the time I spent watching that silly review was not in the least wasted, for I discovered the fundamental reason for my suffering. Do you remember the chicken coop that appeared on stage? The poor birds wanted to sleep. They put their beaks under their wings, but were immediately woken up by the dazzling beams from the spotlights illuminating the "stars", or by the fidgeting of one of their fellow chickens . . . *Well, my soul is just like those poor creatures, constantly being torn from sleep* – or so I realised when I saw them. For all my soul wants is to sleep, but brilliant lights and clamorous voices keep on waking it up: powerful longings, wild ideas, tumultuous aspirations, golden dreams and grey realities. My soul would suffer far less if it never slept. Because what makes this infernal torment worse is that my soul often does manage to drop off, to close its eyes – if you'll forgive the ridiculous phrase. But no sooner does it do so, than someone prods it awake again into bewildered and bleary-eyed pain.'

On another occasion, reminding me of this discovery, he added:

'Lately, for no apparent reason, my moral suffering has become so intense that I am now physically aware of my soul. It's horrible! *My soul does not merely feel anguished, it bleeds.* The moral pain has become actual physical pain, a terrible pain that I can physically feel, *not in my body, but in my spirit.* I know how hard it is for someone else to comprehend this, but believe me, I swear to you it's true. That's what I meant the other night about my soul being constantly wrenched awake. Yes, my poor soul is longing to sleep but they won't let it, it's cold and I don't know how to warm it! My whole soul has grown hard, withered, stiff, so that when I move it – by that I mean, when I think – I suffer horribly. And the harder my soul becomes, the more I want to think! A whirlwind of ideas, mad ideas, drives me to rend it asunder, to snatch at it, to tear it apart, in an act of wild martyrdom! Until one day – it's bound to happen – my soul will simply shatter, fly into a thousand pieces. My poor soul, my poor soul!'

At such moments Ricardo's eyes looked as if they were covered by a veil of light. They did not shine, they were simply veiled in light. I know it sounds odd, but that's how it was.

Still on the subject of the physical pain suffered by his soul, Ricardo suddenly confided to me one afternoon, in a jokey tone he rarely adopted:

'Sometimes, you know, I really envy my legs . . . Because at least a leg doesn't suffer. It has no soul, my friend, no soul!'

When alone, I spent hours thinking about the poet's singular ideas, in an attempt to understand them. But the truth is that I never managed to penetrate his psychology and the only conclusion I reached was this: that he was a superior being, brilliant and disquieting. Even today, after all these years, that is the only thing I am certain of, and that is why I do no more than recount in no particular order – just as I remember them – the most characteristic features of his psychology, as if they were merely documents in my defence.

As I warned at the start, I give facts, only facts.

Our souls understood each other perfectly, insofar as two souls can understand each other. And yet we were two such different creatures. If the truth be told there were few common links between our characters, in fact, the one thing we shared was our love of Paris.

'Ah, Paris!' Ricardo would exclaim. 'Why do I love it so much? I don't know . . . I have only to say to myself that I live in the capital of France for a wave of pride, joy and elation to well up in me. It is the one golden opiate for all my pain – Paris!

How I love its streets, its squares, its avenues! Every time I think of them when I'm far away, they rise up before me like a shimmering mirage, an arching avalanche that floods me with light. And my own body, transfixed, is caught up in the whirl.

In Paris I love everything equally: monuments, theatres, boulevards, gardens, trees . . . To me everything in it has a heraldic, holy significance.

How I suffered the one year that I spent far from my city, with no hope of an early return . . . And my longing then was exactly the same longing you would feel for the body of a lost lover . . .

In the sad evenings I would walk the gloomy streets of south Lisbon saying the name over and over like a prayer: Paris, Paris . . .

And at night, in my great empty bed, before falling asleep, I would remember Paris – yes, remember it – as one might remember the naked flesh of some golden lover!

When I returned to this marvellous city, my immediate, overriding desire was to walk every single one of its avenues, to visit every quarter, the better to entwine myself about her, the better to love her . . . Ah, Paris, Paris!

But, Lúcio, you mustn't think that I love this great city for its boulevards, its cafés, its actresses or its monuments. No, no! That would be vulgar. I love it for some other quality: perhaps because of a kind of aura that surrounds it and constitutes its soul, which I cannot see, but that I can feel, really feel, and yet cannot explain!

I can only live in large places. I so love progress, civilisation, the bustle of people, the feverish activity of modern life! Because, deep down, I love life very much. I'm full of contradictions. I feel desolate, depressed, drained of energy and yet I love life as no one has ever loved it!

Europe! Europe! Rise up within me, fill me with sensation, anoint me with the oils of my own age!

Let them build bridges and more bridges! Let there be railway lines whistling with trains! Let them raise up towers of steel!'

He would get carried away in his own delirium, throwing out increasingly bizarre images, wild ideas.

'Yes, yes! I am one vast contradiction! My own body is a contradiction. Do you think me thin, hunched? I am, but much less so than I seem. You'd be surprised if you saw me naked . . .

But it's more than that. Everyone thinks of me as a man of mystery. For I have no life, I have no lovers . . . I disappear . . . no one knows anything about me . . . All lies, lies! For my life is a life entirely without secrets. Or rather, its secret lies precisely in having none.

And my life, though free of eccentricities, is nevertheless bizarre – but again in a topsy-turvy way. In fact its singularity consists not in the fact that there are elements in it that cannot be found in normal lives, but in its lack of any of the elements that are thought to be common to all lives. That's why nothing ever happens to me. *Not even the things that happen to everyone*. Do you know what I mean?'

I always did. And he did me the justice of believing that I did. That's why our heart-to-heart conversations generally went on into the early hours, as we walked the deserted streets, immune to cold or tiredness, in a state of mutual, flame-bright intoxication.

In quieter moments, Ricardo would speak to me of the sweetness of normal life. And he would confess to me:

'How often, alone in a group of banal acquaintances, I've envied my companions . . . I remember a particular supper at the Leão d'Ouro . . . it was a rainy night in December . . . I was with two actors and a playwright, perhaps you know them: Roberto Dávila, Carlos Mota and Álvares Sesimbra . . . I made a special effort and managed to bring myself down to their level. I even managed to fool myself. Believe it or not, just for a moment, I was happy . . . And Carlos Mota asked me to collaborate with him on one of his operettas . . . Carlos Mota, the author of *Videirinha*, the Trindade Theatre's greatest success . . . They're good fellows. But I'm not like them . . .

Yet ultimately, their life – "the everyday life" – is the only one I love. It's just that I cannot live it. And I'm so proud of not being able to live it . . . I'm so proud of not being happy. Literature has a lot to answer for.'

And then, after a brief pause:

'A close friend of mine, dead now, a friend who had the intense, expansive soul of the true artist, was always surprised to find me rubbing shoulders with certain inferior creatures. It was because *they* were involved in life and I was happy to join them in that illusion. Another of my eternal contradictions! I know that you, the true artists, the truly great souls, never step outside, or even attempt to step outside your golden circle, you never long to descend into life. In that lies your dignity. And you're right. You're far happier. For I suffer doubly, because I live in the same golden circle as you but, at the same time, I also know how to survive down here.'

'I don't agree,' I responded, 'that's what makes you the greater artist. The artists you're referring to wouldn't dare to lower themselves because they sense that were they to brush up against everyday existence, it would suck them in and drown their genius in banality. They're weak, but they are saved by their instinctive knowledge of what would happen to them. Whilst you, my friend, can risk your genius by mixing with mediocrities. Your genius is so great that nothing can corrupt it.'

'That's complete and utter fantasy!' retorted the poet.

'As for being a genius, I wouldn't know . . . What I do know is that the banality of *others* is always something to be regretted. The way the vast majority content themselves with so few longings, so few spiritual desires, so little soul . . . It's heartbreaking! A play by Georges Ohnet, a novel by Bourget, an opera by Verdi, a few lines by João de Deus or a poem by Tomás Ribeiro, that's all they need to fulfill their ideal. But what am I saying? Even those characteristics are the refinements of superior souls. The others – the truly normal – let's not beat about the bush, are content with the sequinned obscenities of some writer of cheap revues lacking even a minimum of grammar.

The *majority*, my dear, the *majority* . . . those poor unfortunates . . . But then, who is to say that they aren't right . . . and all the rest is just nonsense.

Who knows . . .'

Months went by and there was still the same affection between us, the same comradeship.

One Sunday afternoon – how well I remember it – we were walking unhurriedly up the Champs-Elysées, mingling with the crowds, when his conversation veered onto a subject which, up until then, he had never broached, at least not directly:

'Ah, on Sundays in Paris, on these marvellous Sundays, you breathe in life itself, intense, healthy life! It's the simple life, *the useful life* slipping by us, right under our very noses. Hours that we cannot share – we, the ethereal dreamers of beauty, touched by the Beyond, marked by Uncertainty . . . How wonderful! And yet how much better it would be if we were like the ordinary people about us. We would find gentleness and peace, at least in our souls. As it is we have only the light. But the light blinds our eyes . . . We are like alcohol, pure alcohol – *and like alcohol we evaporate in the flame that burns us!*

It's precisely the bustle of this immense city, this present moment, this everyday life that makes me love Paris with such a golden tenderness. Yes, that's the right word, tenderness, a limitless tenderness. I know nothing of affections. Any love I ever felt never went beyond tenderness. I could never love a woman for her soul, that is, for herself. I could only love her for the tenderness that her *kindness* awoke in me, for her fair fingers squeezing mine one sunny afternoon, for the subtle timbre of her voice, for the way she blushed, for her laughter . . . her playfulness . . .

What I find touching about love are things like a white skirt trembling in the air, a satin ribbon plaited by slender fingers, a supple waist, a braid of hair undone by the wind, a song murmured by golden, twenty-year-old lips, a flower whose petals bear the marks of a woman's teeth . . .

No, it is not even beauty that impresses me. It's something vaguer than that, something imponderable, translucent: *kindness*. Oh, but I find that in everything, kindness I mean . . . That's where this giddy longing comes from, a *sexual longing* to possess voices, gestures, smiles, scents and colours!

A mad fire, quite mad! Disastrous!'

But then, growing calmer:

'The good people walking by us, my dear friend, have never known such complications. They live. They do not even think. But I never stop thinking. My inner world has expanded, become infinite, it grows hour by hour. It's horrible. Ah, Lúcio, Lúcio, I'm afraid, afraid of drowning, of losing myself in my own inner world, of disappearing from life, lost in my own world . . .

Now there's a good subject for one of your novels: a man who, by turning in upon himself, disappears from life, emigrates into his own inner world.

You see what I mean? Damned literature . . .'

That afternoon, for no reason whatsoever, I felt in an extraordinarily good mood, free from all worries, but a shiver pricked my flesh, a shiver that always runs through me at crucial moments in my life.

Ricardo was talking again, pointing out to me a superb carriage drawn by two splendid black horses:

'What I'd give to change places with that lovely woman there . . . To be beautiful, really beautiful! To blaze through life, to be one of life's princes. Could there be any greater triumph?

The greatest glory of my life was not – and please don't think it was – any praise that may have been heaped on my poetry, on my genius. No, I'll tell you, it was this: one April afternoon, three years ago, I was walking along one of the great boulevards, alone as usual. Suddenly, a peal of laughter rang out right by me . . . Someone tapped me on the shoulder . . . I ignored them . . . But then they tugged mischievously at my arm with the handle of a sunshade. I turned round. It was two young girls, two charming, smiling girls. They were in fact two seamstresses who had doubtless just left one of the workshops on the Rue de la Paix. They were both carrying parcels. And one of them, the boldest, said:

"You're very handsome you know."

I shrugged the remark off and we walked on together,

exchanging a few banal words. (Believe me I know exactly how ridiculous this confession sounds.)

At the corner of the Rue du Faubourg-Poissonnière, I said goodbye. I had to meet a friend, I said. In fact, some perverse desire made me resolve to put an end to the adventure, afraid, perhaps, that if it went on, I might grow weary of it. I don't know.

We went our separate ways . . .

That afternoon constitutes the most beautiful memory of my entire life!

God, how I long to be beautiful, splendidly beautiful, not the owner of this hunched body, this twisted face! And that afternoon, for a matter of moments, I *was* beautiful, I think. I had just finished writing some of my best lines.

I felt proud, worthy of admiration. The afternoon was blue and bright, the boulevard looked lovely . . . I was wearing a rakish hat, a youthful lock of hair curled upon my forehead . . .

Ah, I lived for weeks and weeks on pure nostalgia . . . I felt filled by tenderness for that young girl whom I never met again – *whom I never could meet again* because, puffed up with happiness, I had not even thought to look at her face . . . How I love her . . . How I love her. How I bless her . . . My love, my dear love!'

Transfigured for an instant, his face lit up by the soft, intense gleam of his dark, Portuguese eyes, Ricardo de Loureiro really was beautiful . . .

Yet even today I could not say if my friend was or was not beautiful. His physiognomy was as contradictory as his personality: for example, seen full on, his long, gaunt face looked radiant, but in profile it did not. But even that was not always strictly true, for sometimes, in certain lights, in certain mirrors, his face, seen from the side, was most attractive . . .

His worst feature though was, without a doubt, his much-despised body, which he simply 'left to its own devices', to use Gervásio Vila-Nova's extravagant, but very apt phrase.

In the pictures of Ricardo that exist today he looks like an extremely handsome man bathed in the glow of genius. But that was certainly not how he normally looked. Knowing they were dealing with a great artist, the photographers and painters gave him an elevated expression that was not typical of him at all. One should always distrust portraits of great men . . .

'Ah, my dear Lúcio,' Ricardo went on, 'how I envy the triumph of a lovely woman, stretched out on a coverlet of lace, contemplating her own naked flesh . . . splendid and golden as alcohol! Female flesh – the apotheosis of beauty! If I were a woman, I would never allow myself to be possessed by the flesh of men – it's so sad, dry, sallow, it has no sheen to it, no light . . . In occasional moments of enthusiasm I feel nothing but admiration and tenderness for the great debauchees, who chose to entwine their marble limbs only about the tawny, sumptuous limbs of others like themselves, other women . . . And I'm filled then by a mad desire to be a woman, for one reason only, in order that I might gaze bewitched upon my own bare, white legs slipping coolly over a linen sheet.'

I was surprised at the turn the conversation had taken. Whilst it was true that Ricardo de Loureiro's work was full of sensuality, of wild perversity, nothing of this ever surfaced in his conversation. On the contrary, his words were untouched by any hint of sensuality – or even tenderness – and he was immediately overcome by embarrassment if, by chance, anything of that nature were even distantly alluded to.

As for my friend's sex life, I knew absolutely nothing about it. Ricardo seemed to me, moreover, quite untroubled in that respect. Perhaps I was wrong. I must have been. And that night I had proof of my mistake – and what proof! – in the strangest, most disturbing and impenetrable of confessions . . .

It was half past seven. We had walked the whole length of the Champs-Elysées and the Avenue du Bois de Boulogne as far as the Porte Maillot. Ricardo decided that we should dine at the Pavillon d'Armenonville, a proposal I accepted with alacrity.

I had always been fond of that celebrated restaurant . . . I don't know why . . . its literary qualities perhaps (for we had read about it in novels), the great red-carpeted salon and the staircase at the rear, the romantic trees shading it, the little lake, all that, combined with the high society atmosphere, evoked for me a distant longing, subtle and shifting, that in turn called up an astral memory of some love affair I had never had, of autumn moonlight, dry leaves, kisses and champagne . . .

... ...

Our conversation ran along simple lines during the meal. It was only when coffee was served that Ricardo said:

'You can't imagine, Lúcio, how your friendship delights me, how I bless the hour that we met. Before I knew you, I had dealings only with indifferent, vulgar creatures who never understood me, not even slightly. My parents adored me, but precisely because of that, they were least equipped to understand me. Whilst you, my friend, have an open, generous soul with enough insight to glimpse my own. That's already a lot. I wish it were more than that, but it is still a lot. That's why today, for the first time ever, I have the courage to confess to you my soul's strangest characteristic, the greatest source of suffering in my life . . .'

He paused for a moment and then, suddenly, in a different tone of voice:

'It's this,' he said, '*I cannot be anyone's friend* . . . Now don't protest . . . I am not your friend. As I said once before, I have never felt affection, only tenderness. For me the greatest friendship would simply be translated into the greatest tenderness. And tenderness always brings with it the desire to touch, the desire to kiss . . . to embrace . . . in a word, to possess. Now, in my case, only after satisfying my desires can I really feel whatever provoked them. The truth, therefore, is that I have never *felt* my own tender feelings, I have only *guessed* at their existence. To feel them, that is, to be someone's friend (since in me tenderness equals friendship) I would be obliged first to possess the person I cared about, be they man or woman. But we cannot possess a creature of our own sex. *Therefore, I could only be the friend of a creature of my own sex, if that creature or I were to change sex.*

You can't imagine the pain it causes me. Everyone can have friendships, they are life's chief consolation, the 'reason' for a whole existence, those friendships that people bestow on us, friendships that we wholeheartedly reciprocate. But, however hard I tried, I would never be able to return any affection: *affections simply do not manifest themselves in me!* It's as if I lacked a sense, as if I were blind or deaf. A whole world of the soul is closed to me. There exists something which I can see but cannot comprehend; something I can touch but cannot feel. Believe me, I am to be pitied, I am a poor wretched man!

At times I feel such self-disgust. Listen. This is the worst part! Face to face with all the people I *know* I should value – *face to face with all the people for whom I sense I feel some tenderness* – I am always gripped by a violent desire to kiss them hard on the mouth! Many a time I've had to suppress the longing to kiss my own mother's lips.

But I haven't told you everything yet – I do not, as you might think, experience these physical desires in my flesh, but *in my soul.* Only with my soul could I quench my tender desires. Only with my soul could I possess those creatures I sense that I value, and thus satisfy, that is, reciprocate my friendships emotionally.

That's all . . .

Don't say anything! Just have pity on me, have pity . . .'

I said nothing. A ragged wind was blowing through my mind. I was like someone walking along a smooth road full of sun and trees at whose feet a fiery abyss had suddenly gaped open.

But, after a matter of minutes, Ricardo exclaimed quite naturally:

'Right, it's time we were getting along.'

And he asked for the bill.

We hailed a hackney cab.

Along the way, as we were crossing some square or other, our ears were assailed by the sound of a violin being played by a blind man, ruining a lovely tune. And Ricardo remarked:

'Do you hear that music? It's like a symbol of my life: a wonderful melody murdered by a terrible, unworthy performer.'

III

We met the following day, as we usually did, but we made no allusion to the previous night's strange conversation. Nor was anything said on the following day, nor ever again . . . not until the final unravelling of my life . . .

However, I could not stop thinking about Ricardo's disquieting confession. Indeed, not a day went by when I did not go over it, almost obsessively, in my troubled mind.

Our friendship continued to grow uneventfully, still in that same spirit of harmony and conviviality of soul. But after ten months, towards the end of 1896, Ricardo, despite his great love for Paris, decided to return to Portugal, to Lisbon, although in fact nothing required his presence there.

We were apart for a year.

During that year, our correspondence was practically non-existent: three letters from me and, at most, two from Ricardo.

Material circumstances and a desire to see my friend again led me, in turn, to leave Paris for good. And in December of 1897 I arrived in Lisbon.

Ricardo was waiting for me at the station.

But how he had changed in the year we had spent apart!

His sharp features had softened, acquired a satiny – indeed, a womanly – sheen and, even more startling, was the fact that his hair was not as dark as it had been, as if its colour had been diluted. Perhaps the fundamental difference I noticed in my friend's physiognomy lay in that change alone – *it had become more diffuse*. That was it, that was my overall impression, that his physical features had become somehow scattered, *diminished*.

His voice had changed too, and his gestures: everything about him, in fact, had grown more shadowy.

I was aware, of course, that recently, during my absence, he had got married. He had written to me about it in his first letter, but only vaguely, without going into details – *as if he were describing something unreal.* For my part, I had replied with some equally vague words of congratulation, without asking to know more, without feeling any surprise at the announcement – as if I too were speaking of something unreal, something I already knew about, *as if it were the predictable dénouement of a play.*

We embraced warmly. He accompanied me to my hotel and it was agreed that I would dine that evening at his house.

Not a word was said about his wife . . . I remember how troubled I felt when, as we reached my hotel, I realised that I had still not asked after her. And so intense was that feeling of disquiet that I could not even bring myself to stammer out one word of enquiry about her, as if I were under some truly inexplicable spell . . .

I arrived. A servant – immaculate to the point of caricature – led me into a large room which, *despite the shafts of light pouring into it*, seemed dark and heavy. In fact, as I entered this resplendent room, I had the same feeling that you get when you come in from the sun into a house plunged in shadows.

I gradually began to be able to make out the objects in the room . . . And then suddenly, without knowing how, as if in a swirl of mist, I found myself sitting on a sofa talking to Ricardo and his wife.

Even now I could not say with any certainty if there was someone already in the room when I entered or if the two of them only appeared after a few moments. Likewise, I have never been able to remember the first words I exchanged with Marta, for that was the name of Ricardo's wife.

I entered that room as if, as I crossed its threshold, I was *returning* to a world of dreams.

That's why my memories of that whole night are so tenuous, although I do not think anything remarkable happened during it. We dined and then, naturally enough, we talked for a long time.

At midnight I took my leave.

As soon as I got back to my room, I lay down and went to sleep. And it was only then that I came to. In fact, as I fell asleep, I had the dizzying impression that I was waking from a prolonged fainting fit, coming back to life. I cannot describe this incoherent feeling any other way, for that was how it was.

(I feel I should emphasise here that I know full well how odd everything I have written must sound. But right from the start I made it clear that my courage would consist precisely in telling the whole truth, however incredible it might seem.)

From then on, I spent many evenings at Ricardo's house. The bizarre feelings I had experienced initially disappeared completely and now I *saw* his wife clearly.

She was a beautiful woman, very blonde, tall and statuesque with firm, subtle, *fugitive* flesh. Her blue eyes seemed always to be gazing nostalgically into the infinite. There was something glorious about all her gestures and she walked with light, silent steps – hesitant but quick. Her face was truly lovely, it had a vigorous beauty, as if carved out of gold. Her hands were disquietingly thin and pale.

She was always sad – though hers was a tormentingly vague sadness – but she was so kind, so gentle and affectionate, that she was, without a doubt, the right companion for Ricardo, the ideal companion.

I almost envied my friend . . .

For six months our existence could not have been simpler or more serene. Indeed those six months constituted the one blissfully happy period of my life.

Barely a day went by without my seeing Ricardo and Marta. A small group of artists used to gather at their house almost every night. Apart from myself, there was the dramatist Luís de Monforte, the author of *Glória*; that most scathing of critics, Aniceto Sarzedas; two twenty-year-old poets whose names I forget; and – most important of all – Count Serge Warginsky, an attaché at the Russian legation, whom we had known slightly in Paris and who, I was surprised to find, was now an assiduous visitor at Ricardo's house. Sometimes, though less frequently, Raul Vilar would appear too, along with a friend – a sad, deranged individual, who now writes turgid novels revealing the intimate lives of his friends, with the intention (he claims) of creating intense, original, disturbing art out of the depiction of unusual psychological states. In fact, he succeeds only in being at once false and obscene.

The evenings passed pleasantly in intellectual – and intensely literary – conversation well spiced with humour provided by Aniceto Sarzedas' unrelentingly savage attacks on his contemporaries.

Marta occasionally joined in our discussions and showed herself to be both highly cultivated and possessed of a sharp intellect. Oddly enough, though, her way of thinking never diverged from that of Ricardo. On the contrary, she always agreed with him, reinforcing what he said, bolstering his theories and opinions with small points of her own.

As for the Russian, he was the sensual one in that group of artists, at least that's the impression I got, I don't quite know why.

Serge Warginsky was a beautiful young man of twenty-five. Tall and slender, he reminded me physically of Gervásio Vila-Nova who, shortly before, had brutally taken his own life by throwing himself under a train. Serge's red lips, wanton and tender, parted to reveal teeth women must have longed to kiss. His reddish-blond hair, parted in the middle, fell gracefully over his forehead and his golden-shadowed eyes never left Marta, or so I was to remember in retrospect. In fact, he, more than Marta, seemed the one truly feminine presence amongst us. (I only acknowledged this strange feeling later, however. During that period of my life, my spirit was quite untroubled by any such extravagant thoughts.)

Serge had a wonderful voice, sonorous, vibrant, fiery.

With a Russian's talent for foreign languages, he was soon speaking Portuguese without even the trace of an accent. Ricardo loved to have him read his poems out loud. Booming forth from that adamantine throat, sound became colour.

It was clear too that Ricardo was very fond of Warginsky. I found him merely irritating – perhaps precisely because of his excessive beauty – so much so that I could not always conceal my impatience when he spoke to me.

The nights I spent alone in the company of Ricardo and Marta were far more agreeable to me, even on those occasions when I was left alone with Marta, for Ricardo would often choose to withdraw to his study.

I would lose myself for hours at a time in conversation with my friend's wife. We felt a lively sympathy for each other, that much was beyond doubt. And it was on those nights that I could best appreciate the intensity of her spirit.

In short, the shadows fell away from my life. Certain otherwise trifling material circumstances had wrought very pleasant changes in me. My latest book, just published, had met with enormous success. Sarzedas himself had devoted a long, lucid article to it, praising it to the skies.

Ricardo, for his part, seemed at his happiest when in his own home.

We had, it appeared, finally reached port. We were, at last, really living.

Months went by. Summer had arrived. The nightly meetings at Ricardo's house had come to an end. Luís de Monforte had gone off to his country estate, Warginsky had left on three months' leave for St Petersburg and the two young poets were somewhere in Tras-os-Montes. The only person who still occasionally put in an appearance was Aniceto Sarzedas, who would turn up in his uniform of monocle and overcoat, complaining about his rheumatism and about the latest publishing sensation.

Ricardo had planned a trip to Norway but in the end decided to stay in Lisbon. He wanted to get a lot of work done that summer, to finish his volume of poems, *Diadem*, which was to prove his masterpiece. And really the best thing to do was to stay in Lisbon. Since Marta was in agreement, that is what happened.

It was around this time that my relationship with my friend's wife became closer; it was a relationship utterly untouched by desire, despite the fact that we spent a lot of time together. Indeed, so anxious was Ricardo to get on with his work that he would leave us immediately after supper and shut up himself up in his study until eleven or twelve o'clock at night.

Besides, despite our closeness, our words were merely part of a detached conversation in which our souls played no part. I would recount to her the plots of future novels, on which Marta would give her opinion, or I would read her what I had just written, always in a spirit of purely intellectual camaraderie.

Up until then I had never entertained any mysterious ideas about Ricardo's wife. On the contrary, she seemed to me very real, very straightforward, very *right*.

But, alas, a strange obsession suddenly began to grow in my spirit.

One night, as if I had woken abruptly from a dream, I found myself wondering:

'*Who exactly is this woman?*'

For I knew nothing about her. Where had she come

from? When had she met Ricardo? It was all a mystery. I had never heard her make the slightest reference to her past. She had never once mentioned a relative or a woman friend. And Ricardo kept the same silence, the same inexplicable silence.

It really was all very peculiar. How had Ricardo met her, he who cultivated so few relationships, who did not even visit the houses of the few friends he had, and how could he have accepted the idea of marriage, an idea he found utterly repellent? *Marriage*. But were they in fact married? I could not even be sure of that. A vague memory surfaced in me: in his letter my friend had never actually said that he had got married. That is, he may have said so, but without ever actually using those exact words. And I realised that when referring to her, he always called her Marta, never 'my wife'.

And it was then that another, even odder fact occurred to me: *that woman had no memories; she never ever spoke nostalgically of some earlier event in her life*. She had never once mentioned a place she had visited, someone she had known, some feeling she had had, in fact, not the slightest thing: not a bow, a flower, a veil . . .

So the disturbing fact was this: the woman presented herself to my eyes as someone who had no past, *who had only a present!*

I tried in vain to drive these fevered thoughts from my mind, but night after night they burrowed deeper into me, my pain becoming focussed on solving the mystery.

In my conversations with Marta I made every effort to force her to return to her past. For example, I would ask her casually about a certain city, if she had many memories of her childhood, if she felt any nostalgia for this or that period of her past life . . . But she – equally casually, I suppose – would elude my questions, more than that, *it was as if she did not understand them*. And, as for me, caught in some incomprehensible spell, I never had the courage to insist – *I felt as awkward as if I had just made an indelicate remark*.

So complete was my ignorance that I did not even know the feelings that bound the two of them together. Did Ricardo really love her? He must. And yet he never told me so, he never spoke of his love for her, which he must certainly have felt. And with Marta it was the same – *as if they were embarrassed to mention their love*.

One day, unable to contain myself any longer – and seeing that I would get nothing out of Marta – I decided to interrogate Ricardo himself.

I managed to blurt out:

'You know, you've never told me how you two met . . .'

I instantly regretted my words. Ricardo went pale, mumbled something inconsequential and then, changing the subject, began outlining for me the plot of a play in verse that he wanted to write.

Meanwhile my *idée fixe* had become a real torment to me and I tried again and again, through both Ricardo and Marta, to shed some light on the matter. All in vain.

But I almost forgot to mention the most peculiar aspect of my obsession.

It was not in fact the mystery surrounding my friend's wife that tortured me. Rather it was the uncertainty: was my obsession real, did it really exist in my mind, *or was it just a dream I'd had and been unable to forget, confusing it with reality*?

I was a mass of doubts now. I believed in nothing, not even in my own obsession. I walked through the ruins of life, even fearing, in my more lucid moments, that I might go mad.

Winter returned and, with it, the artistic soirées at Ricardo's house, the two young bards, lost for ever in Tras-os-Montes, being replaced by a supposed journalist with pretensions to being a playwright and Narciso do Amaral, the great composer. Serge Warginsky, blonder than ever, remained the most assiduous and most irritating of the guests.

I obtained proof of how sick, how very sick, my mind had become on one of those nights, a rainy night in December.

Narciso do Amaral had at last agreed to perform for us his concertante entitled *Beyond*, which he had completed many weeks before but which, until then, only he had heard.

He sat down at the piano. His fingers struck the keys . . .

My eyes had automatically fixed on Ricardo's wife, who had sat down in an armchair towards the back of the room, in a corner, so that I alone was in the position of being able to see both her and the pianist.

A long way from her, at the other end of the room, stood Ricardo.

And then, little by little, as the music grew in marvellous beauty, I saw – yes, actually saw – the figure of Marta slowly fade away, dissolve, note by note, until she had disappeared completely. *All that remained before my horrified eyes was the empty armchair . . .*

... ...

I was suddenly roused from the mirage by the applause of the near-delirious audience who had been transported and deeply moved by the brilliance of the music . . .

Ricardo's voice, husky with emotion, spoke out:

'I found the music quite extraordinary, it aroused emotions in me of an intensity I have never before experienced. It stirred up, as nothing before ever has, troubling, disquieting feelings. It was like the rending of the veil between us and the Beyond, so overwhelming were its harmonies . . . It was as if everything in me that constitutes my soul had to condense down in order to vibrate in sympathy with it . . . I felt it gather anxiously inside me, in a globe of light . . .'

He fell silent. I looked across to where Marta had been . . .

She had come back. She was once more sitting in the armchair.

As I walked back to my house through the insistent drizzle, I felt as if a tumult of fiery, golden claws were whistling about me.

I was adrift in an orgy of mystery, until – in an attempt at lucidity – I managed to attribute the fantastic vision to the immortal nature of the music.

For the rest, I knew only that it had been a hallucination, because it was impossible to explain Marta's strange disappearance in any other way. Besides, given the positions we had occupied in the room, even if her body really had dissolved, presumably I would have been the only one to notice. Indeed, it would have been unusual, in the presence of such powerful music, for someone even to have taken their eyes off its admirable exponent.

From that night onwards, my obsession grew even more intense.

Indeed it seemed to me I might go mad.

Who then was that enigmatic, shadowy woman? Where had she come from, *where had she existed?* I had been talking to her for a whole year and yet it was as if I had never talked to her . . . I knew nothing at all about her, at times I even came to doubt her very existence. And then, I would anxiously run to Ricardo's house, to see her, to reassure myself of her reality, to reassure myself that not everything was madness: *that at least she did exist.*

Ricardo had already more than once noticed something odd about my behaviour. The proof of this was that one afternoon, he solicitously asked after my health. I responded brusquely, I remember, declaring impatiently that there was nothing whatsoever wrong with me and demanding to know where he had got such a ridiculous idea.

And he, astonished at my inexplicable fury, had said only:

'My dear Lúcio, you really must do something about those nerves of yours . . .'

Unable to resist my *idée fixe* any longer, sensing that my mind would go under if I did not manage to throw some light on the mystery and, knowing that I would get nothing out of Ricardo or Marta, I decided to avail myself of whatever other means were open to me.

And that was the beginning of a series of despicable actions on my part, of ill-disguised interrogations of all Ricardo's acquaintances, of all those who would have been in Lisbon at the time of his 'wedding'.

I decided to approach Luís de Monforte first.

I went to his house on the pretext of consulting him about whether or not I should give the go-ahead to a playwright who was thinking of adapting one of my most famous novels for the stage. But, unable to contain my own impatience, I interrupted myself and started asking direct, albeit somewhat vague, questions about my friend's wife. Luís de Monforte listened to them as if bemused, *not because of the questions themselves, but because they came from me*, and he replied in shocked tones, carefully dodging the questions, as if they were indiscretions to which it would hardly be correct for him to respond.

The curious thing was that everyone I questioned reacted in exactly the same way. Only Aniceto Sarzedo was a little more explicit; he rebuffed me with an insult and an obscenity – not in fact an unusual reaction for him.

I felt so humiliated, so shabby, at that moment, I found it hard to have to control my rage and refrain from striking him, to hold out a friendly hand to him when I met him the following night at Ricardo's house.

These clumsy attempts at interrogation were, however, useful to me. For although I learned nothing from them, I did at least reach one conclusion: that no one was astonished at what astonished me, that no one had noticed what I had noticed. For they all listened to my questions as if there was nothing particularly strange or mysterious about the matter at all, they merely reacted as if it were indelicate, even *odd*, of me to touch on the subject. I mean that no one understood my motives . . . And thus I managed to persuade myself that I was in fact wrong.

For a while the clouds lifted from my thoughts and I could once more sit serenely at Marta's side.

But, alas, that time of tranquillity was short-lived.

The only one of Ricardo's acquaintances I had not dared to approach was Serge Warginsky, simply because I felt such antipathy towards him.

However, one night, we met by chance at the Tavares. There was no possible reason why we should not dine at the same table.

And suddenly, in the middle of the conversation, the Russian exclaimed, quite spontaneously, referring to Ricardo and his wife:

'Our friends are such a delight, don't you think? And so friendly . . . I'd met Ricardo before in Paris but our friendship really dates from two years ago, when we were travelling companions. I caught the Sud-Express for Lisbon in Biarritz, they happened to be travelling on the same train, and ever since then . . .'

... ...

IV

Serge's words left me feeling, quite literally, stunned.

Was it possible? *Ricardo had brought her with him from Paris?* But if that were so, how then had I not met her? Had I not accompanied him to the station at the Quai d'Orsay? No, I suddenly remembered, I had not. I was ill at the time, with a terrible bout of flu. And he . . . No, it was impossible . . . it couldn't be . . .

But then, looking further into my memories, I recalled, quite clearly and for the first time, certain obscure details about his return to Portugal.

He loved Paris so much and yet he had decided to go back. *He had told me so and I had not even been surprised* – it was almost as if there were some reason that justified, that demanded that return.

Ah, how I regretted now not having gone with him to the station, regardless of my state of health and regardless of whatever other motive I may have had at the time and since forgotten. Then I remembered that I had in fact been all set to get up, go out and see my friend off, despite having a fever and a raging sore throat . . . In the end though, I gave in to an overwhelming sense of physical torpor and stayed in bed, plunged in a profound lethargy, *a strange, shadowy lethargy.*

... ...

Ah, that woman . . .

Who could she be? Who *could* she be? How had all that happened?

And only then did a rather different memory of Ricardo's letter surface in me, the letter in which I thought I had first learned about his marriage. The truth was that he had made no mention of marriage in that letter, he had made not even a distant allusion to it, he had merely spoken of the 'transformations that had taken place in his life', in his home, and there were phrases that danced before me now in letters of fire: 'now that I have someone with whom to share my life; now that something new has grown out of all that I destroyed . . .'

And the extraordinary thing, I realised then, was that he spoke of all this as if he were describing events I already knew about, events it would be pointless to describe at length, and so he merely mentioned them in passing . . .

But what was even odder was the fact that I, for my part, was not in the least surprised, as if I really had known all about it but had completely forgotten until his letter arrived to nudge me into partial remembrance.

It was true, I wasn't surprised, nor did I say anything to him about my lapse of memory, I asked no questions, it did not even occur to me to do so, *nothing* occurred to me.

The mystery remained then, although now it had taken another direction. That is, the *idée fixe* planted in my mind by that mystery had undergone an essential change.

Before, the mystery had obsessed me simply as a mystery; I had only to solve it for the shadows to fall away from my soul. It was merely a source of anxiety. But now, dear God, the torment had become a compulsion. The secret guarded by that unknown woman drew me on, intoxicated me like champagne – it was the one beautiful thing in my life.

From then on I myself would struggle to maintain it, to protect it from illumination by any light whatsoever. And when it finally crumbled, my pain would be infinite. And if, despite everything, it did dissolve into mere illusion, I might even then still strive to preserve it!

My mind had adapted itself to the mystery and that mystery was to become the framework of my life, the flame and the golden trail . . .

I did not, however, realise this at once, it took me many weeks to learn it and when I did, I recoiled, horrified. I was afraid, terribly afraid. The mystery was that woman. And I loved the mystery.

I loved that woman! I wanted her, I wanted her!

... ...

My God, how I suffered . . .

My spirit was riven by a terrible uncertainty; a continuous shivering fear zigzagged through my flesh. I could not sleep, I could not dream. All about me were only broken lines, pools of muddy light, dissonant noises . . .

It was then, in a burst of willpower, of steely determination, that I began to summon up, with all the lucidity at my command, the strength to leap the abyss, so very near now, towards which I was hurtling . . . I found it at once. What drove me towards that woman, what made me burn with desire for her, was not her soul, not her beauty, it was simply this: her mystery. Once the secret was known, the spell would be broken and I could carry on with my life as before.

I decided to open my heart to Ricardo, to confess to him all my fears, and to ask him to tell *me* everything as well, so that we might put an end to the mystery, so that we might fill in the blank spaces in my memory.

But I was unable to carry out that resolution. I weakened when I saw that I would suffer far more, far more intensely, once the spell was broken, than when I was in its grip.

I summoned up a different courage, the courage to flee.

I disappeared for a whole week, shut up in my house, doing absolutely nothing, spending the whole day walking round and round my room. The notes from my friend began to arrive in shoals and, since I never replied, one afternoon he himself came to find me. They told him I was not at home, but Ricardo paid no heed and rushed into my room shouting:

'What *is* all this about, man? Are you cracking up on me? Come on, get dressed and come home with me this instant.'

I couldn't think of a single reason or excuse. I merely smiled and said:

'Take no notice of me. I'm just in one of my odd moods . . .'

And, at that same moment, I decided not to run away from the abyss any more, but to surrender to the current and let myself be carried wherever it took me. *With that decision I recovered all my former lucidity.*

I went home with Ricardo. At supper the talk was all about my 'eccentric behaviour' and I was the first to make a joke of it.

Marta looked lovely that night. She was wearing a very low-cut black blouse in crepe de Chine. Her tight skirt hinted at the statuesque lines of her legs, which her very open shoes showed to be almost bare but for the curious stockings she wore, made out of metallic threads that crisscrossed to form large diamonds through which her bare flesh showed.

And at supper, for the first time, I sat down next to her when Ricardo gave up his accustomed place, complaining of a draught.

What the following two weeks were like I do not know, though I remained perfectly lucid. No strange ideas troubled my spirit, I felt no hesitation, no remorse. And yet I knew that I was being dragged, deliciously dragged along in a cloud of light that entirely enfolded me and dulled my senses, *that did not let me see my senses*, although I was sure that they were perfectly intact. *It was as if I had put my spirit away in a drawer somewhere.*

... ...

Only two nights after my return, her hands, quite naturally, found mine, for the first time.

Ah, after that, the hours we spent alone together burned magenta red. Our words became – or at least I think they did – mere disconnected phrases, beneath which we hid what we really felt but did not yet wish to reveal, not out of any fear but, quite simply, out of a perverse sensuality.

Then one night, without a word, she guided my fingers to her nipples, which hardened beneath my touch, my fingers crushing the flame-red silk of her kimono.

Every night brought with it a new pleasure, silent and voluptuous.

We would kiss, teeth and lips colliding, she would give me her bare feet to gnaw on, she would let her hair fall about me, or offer up her painted vulva, her lascivious belly covered with dark tattoos, for me to sink my teeth into . . .

And only then, after all these ardent subtleties, all these mad ecstasies – and lacking the strength to prolong our depravities further – did we at last possess each other.

It happened one sad, dark, rainy afternoon in February. It was four o'clock. I had been dreaming of her when, suddenly, she, the enchantress, appeared before me.

I gave a cry of surprise. Marta, however, silenced me at once with a ravenous kiss.

It was the first time she had come to my house and I felt astonished, suspicious of her boldness. But I could not tell her this for she was still kissing me.

... ...
... ...

At last our bodies wrapped about each other, trembling, mad with flame-bright desire.

And the truth is that I did not possess her, it was she, quite naked now, who possessed me . . .

... ...

That night, I dined as usual at Ricardo's house.

I was in a very strange mood. I felt no remorse whatsoever, not even embarrassment or a hint of doubt. On the contrary, I had not felt so well-disposed for ages. Even my friend noticed.

We talked a lot that night, something we had not done for some time. That same afternoon, Ricardo had at last finished his book. And so he stayed on with us after supper . . .

Indeed, so caught up was I in conversation with him, I completely forgot that afternoon's golden events. Looking about me, it did not even occur to me that Marta must have been there with us too . . .

The following morning, when I woke up, I remembered something strange the poet had said to me:

'You know, Lúcio, I had the most bizarre hallucination today. It was in the afternoon, it must have been about four o'clock. I'd just written the last line of my book. I left the study and went up to my room. I happened to glance in the wardrobe mirror but *I wasn't there!* It's true. I saw everything around me reflected in the mirror, *but I could not see my own image* . . . You can't imagine my amazement . . . the mysterious feeling that swept through me . . . But do you know something? It wasn't a feeling of terror, *it was a feeling of pride.*'

However, when I thought about it, I realised that, in fact, my friend had said nothing of the sort. In some very complicated, strange form of recollection, I had merely remembered, not what he had really said to me, but what he should have said.

V

Our affair continued on its unclouded course. I felt elated, proud of my love. I lived like one bewitched, lost in continual wonderment at this white apotheosis of the flesh.

What deliriums shook our mad, flailing bodies . . . how insignificant I felt when she lay her sombre, iridescent self across me, naked and holy!

I walked around in a state of constant amazement at her charms, at my triumph. She was mine! Mine! And so vast was my joy, so great my desire, that at times – as vulgar lovers write in silly, romantic letters – I could not believe my own good fortune; I began to fear that it might all be just a dream.

My relationship with Ricardo remained exactly as before, as did my affection for him. I neither regretted nor condemned what I had done. Besides, having pictured myself in all possible situations, I had already imagined myself in my present circumstances and felt certain that this was how it should be.

Indeed, as I saw it, I had not harmed my friend in any way, I had caused him no pain – nor had he gone down in my esteem in the slightest.

I have never had a conventional attitude towards certain offences, certain moral scruples. I was in no way acting against him.

When I put myself in his place, I could find no reason to feel indignant about what I had done.

Besides, even if it was, in fact, a crime, I was not committing that crime out of malice or with criminal intent. That's why I could not possibly feel any remorse.

All the time that I was lying to him, I felt the same affection for him. Lying does not mean that one loves any the less.

Strangely enough, though, this all-embracing love, this love with no regrets, left me dissatisfied, bruised. It made me suffer terribly.

But, dear God, why? A cruel enigma . . .

I loved her and she loved me, that much was certain . . . she gave herself to me unstintingly. What more did I want?

She was not, like other lovers, prey to sudden caprices, sudden doubts. She neither fled from me nor tormented me.

What was it then that hurt me?

A mystery . . .

The truth is that when I possessed her I felt full of fear, turbulent fear and pain: the pain of elation, a fear veined with confusion, death and terror.

When I was away from her and recalled our ecstasies, I was overcome by an incomprehensible feeling of nausea. And not only when I was away from her. Even at the glorious moment of possession those feelings of repugnance rose up in me and grew in intensity the more my breathless (and undiminished) ecstasy grew, took hold; and, stranger still, I guessed, although I could not know if this was true, that those feelings of repugnance were purely physical in origin.

Yes, when I took her, when I remembered taking her, I always felt a sour aftertaste of sickness, perversity, as if I had possessed a child, a being of another species or a corpse.

And yet her body was a triumph; her glorious body . . . her body exuberant with flesh – aromatic, purifying, tangible . . . salutary . . .

How I fought to ensure that she would not suspect my feelings of repugnance, feelings which – as I said and as I say again – only redoubled and strengthened my desires.

I would stretch myself out upon her naked body, like someone hurling himself into an abyss thronged with shadows, glinting with fire and the blades of knives, or like someone picking up a golden cup, heraldic and ancestral, and drinking down some subtle poison that carried with it an eternal curse.

I began to fear that one day I might strangle her, indeed in moments of incoherent mysticism, the thought whirled into my mind that perhaps this extraordinary woman was simply a demon, an expiatory demon, in some other life into which I had already descended.

And so the afternoons passed.

However hard I tried to attribute my torment to the lie we lived, to our *crime*, I could not deceive myself. I was hurting nothing by my actions, there was no reason for remorse . . . It was all an illusion.

After a time, however, my very desire to plumb the depths of these strange feelings, my long meditations upon them, ultimately inured me to them. And I regained my peace of mind.

But this new period of calm was short-lived. It is impossible to remain calm when confronted by a mystery and I soon remembered that I still knew absolutely nothing about the woman I enfolded in my arms each afternoon.

Even in her most intimate conversations, even in her wildest embraces, she remained utterly sphinx-like. She never once opened her heart to me and continued in her role of the woman with no memory.

When I thought about this later, I realised it was not only her past I knew nothing about, I had my doubts about her present too. What did Marta do during the hours we were not together? It was extraordinary! She had never spoken about it to me, not even to recount to me the smallest episode, one of those futile episodes that all women, that all of us, even the most reserved of us, are always eager to pass on, however mechanically. *It was as if she simply did not exist when she was away from me.*

This idea entered my spirit and I immediately stumbled upon another extremely odd fact:

It seemed that Marta ceased to exist when she was apart from me. But there was more, for when I did not have her by my side, I retained no physical proof of her existence: not a letter, a veil, a dried flower, no portraits, no locks of hair. Only her perfume, which impregnated the sheets on my bed, which danced subtly about me. But a perfume is not real. That was why, as before, I became filled by the old longing to see her, to have her near me in order to be absolutely sure that *she did at least exist.*

When I thought of her, I could never really imagine her. Her features slipped away from me the way the faces of people in dreams do. And, sometimes, when I struggled to remember them, the only features I managed to call up were Ricardo's, doubtless because he was the person closest to her.

I must be possessed of a very strong spirit to have withstood the whirlwind that roared through me then.

(I should point out, however, that these genuine obsessions I describe were never a constant presence in my spirit.

They would disappear for weeks on end and, even at their height, they were worse at some times than at others.)

Along with what I have described, and which constituted the worst of my torments, I was also tortured by other insignificant things, treacherous trifles. I will set down here a curious episode which, though not of any great importance, I believe it would still be useful to mention.

Although we were great friends and very close, Ricardo and I never addressed each other as 'tu', doubtless due to the fact that our intimacy was relatively recent, that we had not been childhood friends. Moreover, this was something we had never even discussed.

However, at that time, I would occasionally find myself calling my friend 'tu'. And when I did so, I would immediately correct myself, *blushing furiously as if I had committed some dreadful gaffe*. And this happened so often that one night, Ricardo remarked quite spontaneously: 'There's no reason to get so embarrassed when you accidentally call me "tu". You don't have to stammer and turn red as a beetroot. That's absurd. Look, from now on, we'll have no more of this formal "você" business. From now on we call each other "tu". It's much more natural.'

And so we did. Nevertheless, I could not help feeling an initial awkwardness when using the new form of address – a form I had been given full permission to use.

Ricardo often made fun of me, turning to Marta and saying:

'He's such an odd fellow this Lúcio . . . Have you noticed? He's like a young bride, pure as a lily . . . a white dove without blemish . . . I don't think!'

There was a reason for my embarrassment, albeit a complex one:

In our intimate conversations, in our embraces, Marta and I called each other 'tu'.

Now, knowing how distracted I had become, I was afraid that at some point I would forget myself and address her as 'tu' in front of Ricardo. This fear finally developed into an obsession and, one day, precisely because I was so afraid that I would, I began to commit sudden lapses. *However, on those occasions, I found myself addressing as 'tu' not Marta, but Ricardo.*

And even though we had both agreed to use that form of address, my feeling of embarrassment continued for a few days afterwards as if, ingenuously, trustingly, Ricardo had demanded that his wife and I call each other 'tu'.

My passionate encounters with Marta always took place at my house, in the afternoon.

Indeed she had never wanted to give herself to me in her own house. There she would offer me only her mouth to kiss and permit me certain other silvery pleasures.

I was astonished at the evident ease with which she was able to get away and meet me every afternoon at the same hour and stay for such a long time.

Once I urged prudence on her. She laughed. I asked her to explain: how was it that Ricardo never questioned her long absences, why did she never seem upset or nervous, walking blithely through the streets, unconcerned about the time? And then she laughed out loud, kissed me on the mouth and fled.

I never again asked her about this. It would have been in bad taste to insist.

However, it was yet one more secret to add to my obsession, to fuel it still further.

Indeed Marta's imprudent behaviour seemed unbounded.

She would often kiss me when we were in her own house, with all the doors wide open, forgetting that we might easily be seen by one of the servants or even by Ricardo himself, who would often emerge unexpectedly from his study. She never worried about that. It was as if such a thing could never happen to us – *it was as if we were not in fact kissing each other.*

Besides, Ricardo was trust personified. You had only to look at him to see that no anxious thoughts tormented him. I had never seen him so contented, so good-humoured.

The vague air of sadness, of bitterness, which still used occasionally to hang over him like a cloud even after his marriage, had disappeared completely, as if, with the passing of time, he had forgotten all about the event whose memory had once caused that faint cloud.

He had told me as soon as I arrived in Lisbon that the

complications of the soul he had once suffered from no longer troubled him, that, in that sense, his life had healed itself.

And, oddly enough, it was immediately after Marta had become my lover that all those clouds had cleared, that I first noticed how well-disposed he was, how proud, jubilant, *triumphant*.

Marta grew more and more indiscreet with each passing day.

As if in the grip of a wild audacity, even Ricardo's presence did not stop her making certain tender gestures towards me!

It made me tremble all over, but he never remarked upon them, *he never saw them*, or if he did, he would merely laugh, or join in.

Thus, one summer afternoon, we were having tea on the terrace when Marta suddenly – in a gesture that could, in fact, have been taken as a simple, playful joke – demanded that I kiss her on the forehead, as punishment for something I had said to her.

I hesitated, turned bright red, but since Ricardo insisted, I bent over, tremulous with fear, and just barely brushed her skin with my lips.

And Marta said:

'Do you call that a kiss! You mean you still don't know how to kiss properly? You should be ashamed of yourself! Come on Ricardo, you show him how to do it.'

And laughing, my friend got up, came over to me, took my face in his hands . . . and kissed me.

... ...

Ricardo's kiss was the same, exactly the same, as my lover's kisses, it had the same colour, the same unsettling effect. Their kisses felt to me identical.

VI

My torment grew worse with each night that passed. And although it was clear that all my sufferings and all my fears had their roots in foolish obsessions and were therefore entirely unreasonable, I nevertheless clung on to one bright certainty: regardless of all that, there *was* a real motive behind the tremor of fear that ran endlessly through me. However foolish my obsessions, my fears were, in the end, justifiable.

Our meetings continued to take place every afternoon at my house and I would await the hour of our embraces trembling, yes, trembling and, at the same time, filled with an agonised longing for the thing that made me tremble.

I had forgotten all my feelings of repugnance, I was troubled now by a different doubt: despite the fact that our bodies had entwined and clung to one another, despite the fact that she had been mine, all mine, for some reason I came to believe that I had never possessed her entirely, as if some physical obstacle prevented me from doing so, *as if she and I were of the same sex!*

And when this wild idea first surfaced in me, I remembered how Ricardo's kiss, that masculine kiss, had felt exactly like Marta's kisses, had had the same colour, the same disquieting quality . . .

... ...
... ...

A few months went by.

Time passed more or less uneventfully. I forgot my disquiet, forgot the mystery, and was engaged in writing a new volume of short stories – my last . . .

All my sad dreams, all the plump notebooks filled with ideas for future projects, I gathered them all together in a spirit of exaltation, but in the end it came to nothing. I was an ethereal builder of towers that were never built, of cathedrals that were never consecrated – poor towers spun out of moonlight . . . poor cathedrals woven out of mist . . .

... ...

Around this time, my crisis entered another very interesting phase, which I must not neglect to mention: during it I thought a lot about my situation, but not as a way of tormenting myself – I did it coldly, disinterestedly, as if it had nothing whatsoever to do with me.

I decided to re-examine the beginning of our affair. How had it started? I could not remember. Strange though it may seem, the truth is that I had forgotten all the little episodes that must have preceded it. For we had certainly not begun at once with kisses, with lascivious caresses – there must have been some hesitation beforehand which I could not now remember.

And I had forgotten those episodes so completely that I had no sense of having forgotten them: recalling them seemed an impossibility, as impossible as remembering things that had never happened . . .

But, I repeat, these bizarre events did not cause me any pain; during this period I was able to stand outside myself, in a state of fascination, of lucid fascination, from which at the time I drew my consolation.

All I could remember – or at least so I told myself – was the first time that our hands had touched, our first kiss. Not even that much. It was rather that I knew there must have been a first touching of hands, a first meeting of lips . . . the way it happens in novels . . .

When the memory of that first kiss was at its clearest, it always seemed to me the most natural, least wicked thing in the world, even though it had been a kiss on the mouth. On the mouth? But I was not even sure of that. On the contrary, it was quite possible that the kiss had been on my cheek, like Ricardo's kiss, *the kiss that so resembled Marta's kisses.*

My God, if I had known then that I was only at the

halfway point of my calvary, that all I had suffered up until then would be as nothing in comparison with the torment to come, this time a very real torment, not a mere obsession . . .

One day I noticed a slight change in Marta's attitude, in her gestures, in her face, a vague constraint, a peculiar distraction, doubtless due to some worry troubling her. At the same time I noticed that she did not give herself to me with quite the same intensity.

She no longer spent quite so many hours at my house and then, one afternoon, for the first time, she failed to appear at all.

The following day, she made no reference to her absence and I dared not ask her about it.

Meanwhile, I noted that the expression on her face had changed again, her look of melancholy serenity had returned, but it was a different serenity, mellower, softer, more sensual . . .

And from then on her absences became more frequent, or else she would arrive outside our usual hours, coming in only to leave again, without our making love.

Thus I lived in a state of constant torment. I got up each day terrified that she would not come. And from the morning onwards I would wait for her, shut up in my house, in a state of uncontrollable excitement that exhausted me, burned me.

For her part, Marta never thought to justify her absences or her rebuffs. And I, however much I wanted to, however ardently I wanted to, never dared ask her the slightest thing.

I should also explain that our closeness had ended the moment our affair began. In fact, from the moment Marta was mine, I looked at her the way one looks at someone far superior and to whom one owes everything. I had received her love as if it were alms given by a queen, as if it were the last thing I could have expected, *an impossibility*.

For that reason I never risked uttering a word.

I was merely her slave, a slave for whom, she, the

corrupt patrician had prostituted herself. But precisely because of that, the anxiety gripping me only redoubled in strength.

... ...

One afternoon I came to a decision.

It was long past the hour at which Marta used to arrive but now never did.

'What would she be doing at that moment? Why had she not come?!'

I had to find out something, anything.

When she had failed to turn up on previous occasions, I had more than once been on the point of going out to look for her. But I had never dared leave my room, filled by the childish fear that, however late it was, she might still appear.

On that day, however, I overcame my fears. I decided to act . . .

I ran to Ricardo's house aflame with longing.

I found him in his study, amidst an avalanche of papers, making a selection of his unpublished poems for a two-volume edition – a task he had been labouring over for more than a year.

'Thank heavens you're here!' he cried. 'Now you can help me with this ghastly job.'

I turned to him, stuttering, not daring to ask after his wife, the only reason for my unexpected visit. Was she at home? It seemed unlikely. Although she might be . . .

I only saw her at supper. She was dressed in a tailored suit, as if she had been out for a walk . . .

... ...

All my obsessions dissolved, to be replaced by jealousy, a jealousy I concealed from my lover as if it were something to be ashamed of, a jealousy I did my best to hide from myself, trying hard to replace it with my old imaginings. But always in vain.

Nevertheless, never more than three days passed without Marta coming to me.

The physical horror her body had once aroused in me had returned. However, that horror, combined with my jealousy, only made me desire her all the more, mottling my ecstasies with tawny colours.

On the afternoons when she did not come to me, I often repeated the experiment of hurrying round to her house. But I always found Ricardo there. Marta appeared only at supper . . . And, in my incredible timidity, I never asked after her, I somehow forgot to do so, as if that were not in fact the sole reason I had gone to see my friend at that hour.

One day, Ricardo remarked on my untimely visits, on my feverish appearance when I arrived, and from then on, I never again repeated the exercise, which was, anyway, pointless.

I decided to spy on her instead.

One afternoon I hired a coupé and ordered the driver to wait near her house. I sat inside with the curtains drawn. I waited for some time. At last she came out. I told the driver to follow her at a distance.

Marta walked down a sidestreet, then turned left up an avenue parallel to the one she lived in and where there were still only a few houses. She stopped at a small building with a façade of green tiles. She went in without knocking.

... ...

God, how I suffered! I had followed her in search of proof that she had another lover. I must have been mad. For then, even if I had wanted to, I could no longer delude myself.

And how deceived I had been before to think I would not care if my lover betrayed me in the flesh, that it would matter little to me if she belonged to others.

Then began my final torment . . .

I made an entirely fruitless effort to forget what I had

discovered, to hide my head beneath the sheets the way children do on winter nights, for fear of thieves.

When I embraced her, I flew into such wild ecstasies, bit her so passionately, that once she cried out.

Indeed, whilst it wounded my very soul to know she was possessed by another lover, it also excited me, inflamed my desire . . .

Yes – the truth flickered before me in livid purple – that splendid, glorious body had given itself to three men, three males had covered it, profaned it, drunk of it. Only three? Perhaps a whole multitude. And even while that idea was still lacerating my mind, I was also filled by a perverse desire for it to be true.

When I clutched her convulsively to me, it was in fact as if, with my monstrous kisses, I was also possessing all the male bodies that had passed through hers.

I became obsessed with finding on her flesh some mark, some wound left by love, some trace of one of her other lovers.

And, at last, one triumphant day, I found a great black bruise on her left breast. On an impulse, I glued my mouth furiously to that mark, sucking, biting, tearing at it.

Marta, however, did not cry out. Nothing would have been more natural than for her to cry out at my violence, for I could even taste blood in my mouth. But she made not a murmur. She seemed not even to notice that brutal caress.

When she left, in fact, I was unable to recall that kiss of fire, some strange doubt would not allow me to remember it.

... ...

Ah, what I would have given to know her other lover . . . her other lovers.

If she would only speak to me of her love affairs freely, sincerely, if I knew where she was and when, all my jealousy would disappear, would have no further reason to exist.

Indeed, if she did not hide these things from me, *if she only hid them from the others*, that would give me primacy. I would feel only pride then and there was no way I could rebel out of pride. Because, I realised, that was the truth: my suffering came only from my wounded pride.

No, I had not deceived myself before, when I thought that I would feel no pain if my lover gave herself to others. She had only to tell me all about her love affairs, even about the pleasure her other lovers gave her.

It was the secrecy my pride could not bear. And Marta was all mystery. That was the main source of my anxiety, *of my jealousy*.

I often tried to make her understand what I wanted, to show her how I felt, to see if I could wrench from her some wholehearted confession, thus bringing my torment to an end. She, however, either did not understand me or her affection for me was too slight for her to give me such proof of her love.

Whilst all my other obsessions had foundered in the face of my jealousy, I was, as I said before, still struggling with my incomprehensible feelings of repugnance.

And in a fresh attempt to explain them to myself, this fearful thought suddenly seized me: *could they have their origins in the other lover?*

Let me explain:

I have always been prone to great physical, purely external antipathies. I remember, for example, an Italian girl, who frequented the Paris restaurant where I dined nightly with Gervásio Vila-Nova; she was a really lovely creature – no doubt an artist's model – to whom I felt very drawn, for whom I almost came to feel desire.

But such feelings soon died.

One Sunday I saw her walking along hand in hand with a man I found deeply tedious and whom I knew spent every afternoon playing cards in a bourgeois café in the Place Saint-Michel. He was the image of what maids and ladies in their forties call 'a nice boy'. He was very pale and blond, with pink cheeks and a small, perfectly curled moustache. He had curly hair, long eyelashes and a tiny mouth, as soft as if sculpted in butter. In manners and gestures he was unctuous, like a cashier in a dress shop – he certainly looked the part!

I took such an intense dislike to this saccharin creature that I never returned to the parochial little café in Place Saint-Michel. I literally could not bear to be in his presence. I always felt like throwing up in his face, for he provoked exactly the kind of nausea that a vile mixture of rancid bacon, chicken fat, honey, milk and aniseed might cause.

When I came across him – which happened quite often – I could not conceal my feelings of irritation. For example, I missed lunch one day simply because, just as I was taking my seat in a restaurant I did not normally frequent, the presumptuous fellow had the nerve to come and sit down opposite me, at the same table. I was seized by an urge to slap him in the face, to flatten his little nose beneath a rain of blows. I restrained myself, however, paid my bill and left.

Seeing that fashionable young lady holding hands with such a fool was tantamount to seeing her drop dead at my feet. She remained as delightful as ever, of course, but after that I could never again even bear to talk to her. The blond young man had soiled her, besmeared her, for ever. Had I kissed her, his buttery image would immediately have reared up before me, I would have been overcome by the damp taste of saliva, of sticky, viscous things. Actually to possess her, then, would have been like bathing in a murky sea covered in yellow scum, bobbing with straw, melon skins and bits of cork.

Anyway, what if my feelings of repugnance towards

Marta's lovely body had the same origin? What if the lover about whom I knew nothing were someone who, had I known him, would fill me with disgust? That could well be the case, an accurate presentiment, especially since – as I have already mentioned – when I possessed her I often had the monstrous feeling that I was also possessing the masculine body of that lover.

But the truth is that, deep down, I was almost certain I was still deceiving myself, that the man involved was very different, that the reasons behind my mysterious feelings of repugnance were far more complex. Or rather, that even if I met her lover and disliked him, that would not be the cause of my nausea.

In fact her flesh did not repel me in the sense that it made me feel sick, her flesh filled me rather with a sense of monstrousness, of *strangeness*. I felt sickened by her body in the same way I had always felt sickened by epileptics, madmen, witches, seers, kings, popes – people marked by mystery.

In a final act of will I decided I would make one last attempt to extract an explanation from Marta by giving her a frank description of all my torments or, if that failed, by insulting her. I needed to put an end – whatever form that might take – to my hellish situation.

But I never managed to do so. Whenever I opened my mouth to speak, I would look into her infinite eyes . . . and her gaze would hold me fascinated. And like a medium in a hypnotic state, I would come out with other words instead – *perhaps the words she obliged me to speak.*

Finally, I resolved somehow to find out who lived in the small green house. I detested such underhand behaviour but I had, after all, already sunk to following Marta.

So I screwed up my courage and decided to ask for information in the neighbourhood, even, in the last instance, from the porter's lodge of the house itself – assuming there was one.

I chose a Sunday morning for my investigations, a day when Marta and I normally met at her house, for on Sunday afternoons Ricardo always took us for a drive in his car which at the time – the year was 1899 – still caused something of a sensation in Lisbon.

However, as I turned into the sidestreet that led to the avenue in which the mysterious building stood, I encountered a setback: Ricardo was walking immediately ahead of me. I could not hide. He had already seen me, though how I don't know.

'What are you doing here at this time in the morning?' he cried in surprise.

I summoned up all my strength and stammered out:

'Ah, yes . . . I was on my way to your house and I just thought I'd come and have a look at these new streets . . . I was feeling fed up . . .'

'What, with the heat?'

'No . . . But what about you? You don't usually go out in the mornings, especially not Sunday mornings.'

'Oh, the usual stupid reason. I'd just finished writing a poem and in my desire to read it to somebody, I was on my way to Serge Warginsky's house to show it to him. It's just near here. Why don't you come with me? We can kill time before lunch.'

At these words a shiver ran through me. Silently, mechanically, I fell into step with him.

Ricardo broke the silence:

'So, how's your play coming along?'

'I finished it last week.'

'What! But you never said a word to me about it!'

I excused myself, murmuring:

'I must have forgotten . . .'

'That's the devil of an excuse!' I remember him saying, with a laugh. Then he went on:

'But tell me now, are you happy with the play? How did you resolve that difficulty you had in the second act? Does the sculptor still die?'

And I said:

'It all turns out fine. The sculptor . . .'

I broke off suddenly; we had reached the small green house.

No, it wasn't an illusion: opposite us, on the other side of the road, Marta was walking along with her usual light step – hesitant but simultaneously brisk and silent. Unaware of our presence, unaware of anything about her, she was making straight for the mystery house, knocking on the door this time before entering.

And, at the same moment, Ricardo suddenly caught my arm and said:

'There's really no point us bothering Serge. What I want to hear about is your play. Let's go to your house now and get it. I want to hear it this afternoon, especially since the car needs mending, there seems to be some new thing wrong with it practically every other day . . .

... ...

I lived through the whole of the rest of that day as if wrapped in a dense cloak of fog. I nevertheless managed to read my play to Ricardo and Marta. Yes, when we got back to their house again, having first gone to mine, Marta was already back, *and I noticed that she had even changed her dress*, although, contrary to her usual custom, she was wearing, not an indoor dress, but an outfit for walking.

I remember too that all the time I was reading my play, I had only one clear thought: how odd it was that I, in my state of mind, could still manage to function normally.

Besides, as I remarked earlier, my pains, anxieties and obsessions were intermittent, they came and went, just as during times of social unrest, daily life goes on amidst the cannon shot and the shooting in the squares, so I went on with my intellectual life in the midst of my torment. That is precisely why up until then I had succeeded in hiding from everyone the tribulations of my soul.

But along with the one clear thought I described above, another extremely bizarre thought occurred to me whilst I read. It was this: it seemed to me vaguely that *I* was my play – that is, the artificial thing – and my play was real.

A parenthesis:

Anyone who has followed me so far must, at least, acknowledge my impartiality, my complete frankness. Indeed, in this simple exposition of my innocence, I never avoid describing my obsessions, my apparent contradictions, which, interpreted narrowly, might lead one to conclude not that I am guilty, but that I am a liar or – taken to its logical extreme – mad. Yes, *mad*, I'm not afraid to write the word. Let me make that absolutely clear, since I need all the credit I can for the end of my story, so mysterious, so outlandish is that end.

Ricardo and Marta congratulated me warmly on my play – I think. But I can't be sure, due to the dense cloak of grey fog that enfolded me, allowing me only those few clear memories I have mentioned.

I dined with my friends but left early saying I was feeling slightly unwell.

I hurried back home and went immediately to bed. But before going to sleep, I went over the key scene of the day and remarked on this strange fact:

When we stopped opposite the green building, I saw Marta walk nonchalantly up to the door and knock . . . Now, given the direction from which she had appeared, she must have been walking behind us all the time. Therefore, she must have seen me: *therefore I must have seen her* when, opposite a large building under construction – I remembered this clearly – I looked back . . . And at the same time – I can't recall why – I remembered that my friend, when he suddenly decided not to go to Warginsky's house, had finished his sentence with these words:

'. . . the car needs mending, there seems to be some new thing wrong with it practically every other day.'

And those were the only words I could remember clearly, indeed the only words I was sure I had heard him say. And yet they were the only words I could not believe he had spoken . . .

I spent further long hours going over the whole peculiar day. But at last I fell asleep and slept until late the next morning.

... ...

Two days later, without telling anyone, without even writing a note to Ricardo, I *finally* had the courage to leave . . .

Ah, the relief I felt when I at last got out at the station on Quai d'Orsay: I could breathe again, my soul unknotted.

I've always experienced the moral sufferings of my soul as physical pain. And the awful impression that had long dominated my life was this: that my soul had become bent, twisted, confused . . .

But then, finding myself far from everything that had troubled me, that strange pain vanished. I felt my spirit slowly untangle.

In my anxiety to reach Paris, my torments had, in fact, intensified during the journey. I thought that I would never reach Paris, that I could not possibly have triumphed, that I must be dreaming, or else that I would fall into some ambush on the way, that they would force me to return to Lisbon, that hard on my heels would be Marta, Ricardo, along with all my friends, all my acquaintances . . .

And a tremor of horror zigzagged through me when, on entering Biarritz, I saw a tall, blond man, whom for an instant I took for Serge Warginsky. But when I looked at him properly – *looked at him properly for the first time* – I smiled to myself: all the stranger had in common with the Russian count was his height and his blond hair.

... ...

Back in Paris, once I had crossed the monumental, aristocratic Place de la Concorde, sparkling with lights, I could doubt it no longer, *I had succeeded.*

Again, I plunged back into Europe, let its atmosphere take possession of me, and Paris rose up within me again – *my Paris,* the Paris I had first known when I was twenty-three.

Those were to be the last six months of my life.

I lived them day to day, unhurriedly, going to cafés, theatres, the best restaurants . . .

During the first few weeks – and even occasionally later on – I still thought about my situation, but never obsessively.

In the end – I sensed – it was all much simpler than I had imagined. The *mystery* of Marta? Well, people do get up to the most extraordinary tricks . . . adventuresses are ten a penny . . .

And it even occurred to me that, if I wanted to, by making a huge effort, by dint of great concentration, I could simply resolve to give up trying to explain it and instead just forget about it completely. *For when you forget something, it's as if it never existed.* If I managed to wipe that sad episode from my memory, it would be exactly as if it had never happened. And that is what I tried to do.

I could still not stop myself thinking about one aspect of the affair: Ricardo's astonishing complacency – *his shameless complacency*. Had things reached such a pitch that his wife could follow him, almost accompany him, to her lover's house? For if we had not seen her, she, however distracted she might have appeared as she walked along, must have seen us. *But even that had not made her turn back!*

And a whirl of tiny incidents crowded into my mind, a thousand facts that were, at first glance, unimportant, a thousand insignificant details I had only just noticed.

My friend must have known about it all for a long time now; he must have known about our relationship . . . He could not have done otherwise. Not unless he was blind. It was horrifying!

And yet he was the one who always wanted me to sit at his wife's side. He had changed places at the table, on the pretext of some non-existent draught, just so that I might sit next to Marta and her legs entwine with mine.

When the three of us went out together, I walked beside her . . . And on our drives in the car, Ricardo was always at the wheel and we two would sit alone in the back . . . close together . . . *holding hands.*

For our fingers would immediately interlace, mechanically, instinctively. It was inconceivable that he had not noticed when, as he often did, he turned round to say something to us.

But the odd thing is that at those moments I was never

afraid that he would see us, it never troubled me, I never made the slightest attempt to unclasp my hand from hers. It was as if our hands were not in fact clasped together and as if we were in fact sitting far apart.

And would the same thing happen with Serge? Of course . . . *Ricardo held him in such high esteem.*

... ...

The most shameful, most unbelievable fact was that, *knowing all this*, his friendship, his affection, towards myself and towards Serge, nonetheless grew with each day that passed . . .

That he should know and yet keep silent, because he loved his wife so much and was, above all, afraid of losing her, was just about admissible. But in that case he should at least have shown a more noble attitude, not heaped praise and affection on us . . .

It revolted me! Not his attitude so much, as his lack of pride. I have never been able to forgive a lack of pride. And I felt that my entire friendship with Ricardo de Loureiro was foundering in the face of his baseness! Yes, his baseness! And he was the one who had so often declared to me that pride was the one quality whose absence he could never forgive in a person.

But there is something I should clarify: when I thought about my friend's extraordinary behaviour, I was never tormented by memories of my old obsessions. I had forgotten them completely. Even if I had remembered them, I would have given no importance whatsoever to the *mystery* – undoubtedly a very shoddy *mystery* – to my jealousy, or to anything else . . .

Just occasionally, I would be filled with, at most, a vague nostalgia, diluted by melancholy, for everything that had once tormented me.

We always react the same way: time passes and everything becomes a source of nostalgia for us – suffering, disillusion, even pain . . .

Indeed, even now, on bleak afternoons, I cannot help

but feel a kind of mauve nostalgia for a sweet, distant memory, for a certain hesitant young creature I never knew and who barely touched my life. And for one reason only: because she kissed my fingers and, one day, smiling, before all our friends, secretly placed her firm, bare arm upon my hand.

And then she fled from my life, just slipped away, although I, out of pity – mad creature that I was! – still longed to gild her with my golden self, out of some melancholy tenderness provoked by her caresses.

And I suffered . . . she was utterly insignificant, but I really suffered . . . wounded by tenderness, a very mild tenderness . . . penetrating . . . aquatic.

My affections always found expression in feelings of tenderness . . .

However, when that sweet nostalgia for my former sufferings stirred in me, that is, a nostalgia for Marta's naked body, it would vanish the instant I recalled Ricardo's shameful response.

And my feelings of revulsion grew ever stronger.

Fortunately, I had received no letter from him. If I had, I would not even have opened it.

No one knew my address. From chance meetings with vague acquaintances, they would know at most that I was in Paris.

I never bought a Portuguese newspaper; if there was any news about Lisbon in *Le Matin*, I made a point of not reading it and thus I almost succeeded in forgetting who I was . . . Amongst the cosmopolitan crowd, I became someone without a fatherland, without ties, without roots anywhere in the world.

On my solitary walks along the boulevards, along the avenues and across the broad squares, a strange desire would arise in me: 'Ah, how happy I would be to have been born nowhere and yet still exist . . .'

One afternoon, I was, as usual, leafing through the latest literary novelties in one of the shops in the Odéon district, when I came across a volume in a yellow jacket, just published, according to the customary red sash. And before my eyes, in letters of fire, there blazed the name of Ricardo de Loureiro . . .

It was, in fact, the French translation of *Diadem*, which an enterprising publisher had just produced, revealing a new literature to the world . . .

... ...
... ...

That afternoon, for the first time since I had arrived back in Paris, I spent a few truly mad hours.

During them I plunged into thoughts of Ricardo, his inexplicable behaviour, his unforgivable lack of pride.

I brooded on all the minor episodes I have described above, I recalled other more significant ones, losing myself again in my desire to discover the identity of all Marta's possible lovers. And in a wild moment, I came to believe that every single one of the men I had ever seen at her side had also passed through her body – *and with her husband's knowledge*: Luís de Monforte, Narciso do Amaral, Raul Vilar . . . all of them, every single one.

Meanwhile, in the midst of all this, there was something still more bizarre: it was that, mingled in with all that revulsion, disgust and hatred – yes, hatred – for Ricardo, was a kind of vague resentment, a jealousy, a real jealousy of him. *I envied him!* I envied him because *she* had belonged to me . . . to me, to the Russian count and to all the others!

And so strong was the feeling that afternoon that, in a flash, the absurd idea flew into my head that I should murder him – to satisfy my envy, my jealousy: *to avenge myself on him!*

... ...

But I finally calmed down and the only feelings I had then for my former friend were my disgust, my anger and a burning desire to throw back in his face his own lack of dignity, his baseness, to scream at him:

'Look, we were *all* her lovers . . . me and all of us, do you hear? *And we know that you know!*

That night, before going to sleep, this disturbing idea came to me in a kind of luminous haze:

'His baseness . . . his lack of pride . . . Ah, but I'm wrong, I'm wrong . . . it's Marta who tells him everything . . . he only knows all about it because *she* tells him . . . she keeps secrets from everyone but him . . . as I wanted her to do with me . . . the way I wanted *her* just for me . . . In that case . . . in that case . . .'

And at the same time – terrifyingly, nonsensically – the memory surfaced in me of the strange confession Ricardo had made to me one night, years ago now . . . after supper . . . in the Bois de Boulogne . . . in the Pavillon, the Pavillon d'Armenonville . . .

VII

It was early October 1900.

One afternoon, in the Boulevard des Capucines, someone suddenly called to me, clapping me on the shoulder:

'There you are! Just the man I wanted . . .'

It was Santa-Cruz de Vilalva, the great impresario.

He took my arm and forced me to sit down next to him on the terrace of Café La Paix. He then began berating me with the bewilderment my disappearance had caused him, especially since I had been speaking to him about my new play only days before I vanished. He said that a lot of people in Lisbon had asked after me, that they had only found out I was in Paris through some Portuguese people who had come up for the Exhibition. In short, he said: 'What the devil are you playing at? You're not cracking up, are you?'

As always happened when someone questioned me about the way I lived my life, I became confused – I blushed and stammered out some excuse or other.

The great impresario interrupted me, exclaiming:

'Fine. But before we do anything else, let's get straight to the point: give me your play.'

I said that I hadn't finished it yet, that I wasn't satisfied with it . . . to which he replied:

'I'll expect you tonight at my hotel . . . the Hôtel Scribe . . . Bring me the play. I want to hear it today. What's the title?'

'*The Flame*.'

'Excellent. See you later then. The premiere will be in April. The last play of the season. I need to close on a high note.'

I found that meeting, which brought an end to my six months of isolation, most unpleasant. Yet, at the same time, I didn't really mind. Literature raised its head again . . .

I hadn't written a single line since I arrived in Paris – I no longer even thought of myself as a writer. And now, suddenly, I was reminded of it, given proof of the esteem in which my name was held and by someone I knew to be little given to flattery, someone indeed who was always brusque and business-like.

That night, as agreed, I read my play. Santa-Cruz de Vilalva was exultant: At least thirty performances, guaranteed, he'd bet his life on it. 'My best play yet,' he assured me.

I handed over the manuscript to him, but on the following conditions:

I would not attend rehearsals nor would I be involved in casting or in any discussions about the *mise en scène*. In fact I would have nothing whatsoever to do with it. I would leave everything to him. Most important of all, he must on no account write to me about it.

The great impresario agreed to everything. We chatted for a while longer and then, as we were saying goodbye, he said:

'By the way, do you know who else has been asking after you, wanting to know if I had any news of you, of your address? Ricardo de Loureiro. He said you hadn't written to him once since you left. I'm putting on a play by him too . . . a play in verse . . . Goodnight.'

I had forgotten all about my meeting with the impresario, about my play, everything, I had plunged back into my former state of indifference, when I suddenly had a new idea for the last act of *The Flame*, entirely different from my original one, a really fine idea that I felt genuinely excited about.

I could not rest until I had written the new act. And one day I could resist no longer and I left for Lisbon, taking the new version with me.

When I arrived, rehearsals had only just begun.

The actors embraced me effusively and Santa-Cruz de Vilalva said:

'I knew you'd turn up. We know what you writers are like. You're all the same.'

The rehearsals were going very well. Roberto Dávila, in the role of the sculptor, was clearly set to give one of his finest performances.

Two days went by.

The astonishing thing was that, contrary to all my plans, contrary to my own wishes, I had not yet mentioned the new act I had written for the play, my sole reason for returning to Lisbon.

However, on the third day, I got up my courage (quite rightly, I needed all the courage I could muster) and told the impresario what had brought me all the way from Paris.

Santa-Cruz de Vilalva asked to see the manuscript but would not let me read it to him.

When he met me the following morning, he bellowed at me:

'You're mad, man! The original work is a masterpiece. With respect, this . . . Can I give you my frank opinion?'

'Of course,' I said, worried.

'It's utter tripe!'

I was filled with rage at the impresario's rudeness, at his lack of insight. If I had ever felt a flicker of genius in my work, it was in those pages. I managed to control myself.

I don't quite know what happened next. The fact is that the play was withdrawn from rehearsals, since I would not allow it to be performed with the original act and, on the advice of the director and the leading actors, the company flatly refused to put it on with the new act.

I broke off relations with all of them and demanded that they return to me all copies of the manuscript as well as any copies of the parts. This request was thought odd – I remember this clearly – especially given the vehemence with which I made it.

When I got home, I threw everything, including the original manuscript, into the fire.

Such was the fate of my last play.

Several weeks went by.

The physical aches and pains I used to suffer in my spirit had returned, but now the pains had no justification, at least none I could think of.

Since arriving in Lisbon I had not, of course, looked up any of my friends. Sometimes I even got the impression that people I had known before were avoiding me. They were writers, playwrights, journalists, who doubtless wanted to flatter the great impresario on whom they all depended or one day would depend.

Only one thing surprised me: Ricardo had made no attempt to seek me out, although, at the same time, this seemed perfectly understandable, quite natural really. He had no doubt understood the reasons for my withdrawal and so, very sensibly, had kept his distance.

I was very glad he had chosen that path. If not, there would have been a most unpleasant scene between us. Face to face, I would not have been able to bite back my insults.

The Flame affair had really upset me. I felt a tremendous wave of disgust for the whole commercial side of art. For it was commerce alone that had condemned the new version of my play. Instead of being merely theatrical with a tight but slick plot, as in the original text, the new version was profound and disturbing, it rent the veil concealing the Beyond.

In a mood of terrible vexation I took to spending whole days randomly wandering the streets of the city, preferably streets in Lisbon's farthest-flung districts.

I remember walking along avenues, turning off down sidestreets, feeling anxious, almost breaking into a run, like someone, in fact, vainly seeking someone he very much wants to find – I don't know why, but that was the comparison that sometimes came to mind.

Generally, I would return home early, as soon as it grew dark, feeling feverish, exhausted, stunned, and sleep the sleep of the dead until morning came and I could begin my wanderings again.

The odd thing is that during that time I never thought to return to Paris, to that calm state of isolation of the soul, not because that way of life no longer appealed, the idea simply never occurred to me.

Then one day I saw someone crossing the road, coming in my direction.

I wanted to run away, but my feet were rooted to the spot. Ricardo himself was standing before me.

I can't remember now the first words we exchanged, doubtless because they were so banal. Ricardo probably spoke of the alarm my disappearance and my present behaviour had caused him.

Whatever it was he said, he spoke in a tone of great sadness and there was a look of real pain on his face. His eyes may even have been shining with tears as he told me all this.

Seeing him there before me, I, for my part, found myself unable even to think. It was as if a dense veil of fog had wrapped about me, as it had that last afternoon I had spent with my friend.

I listened in silence to his complaints, until, suddenly – unfettered, wide awake – I could control myself no longer and, as I had feared would happen, I began screaming out my hatred at him, my revulsion, my disgust.

His pained expression did not change with my words,

he did not even seem surprised, as if I had responded perfectly naturally to what he had said. But then the tears started to flow down his cheeks, *though the pain that caused them was no different from the earlier pain.*

I ended my tirade with the words:

'I had become stuck fast in the mud. That's why I fled, I couldn't bear the shame. Do you hear? Do you?'

He trembled all over then. A shadow crossed his face.

He stopped for a moment and then, at last, in a very strange, barely audible voice, hoarse with tears, so peculiar it did not even seem to issue from his throat, he said:

'You're so wrong . . . My poor friend! My poor friend! I was so thrilled with my success. It never occurred to me that other people wouldn't understand. Listen to me! Listen to me! *You must listen to me!*'

Will-less, drained, silent, I followed him as if drawn along by threads of gold and light, while he explained himself to me:

'Yes, Marta was your lover, and not only yours. But I never knew who her lovers were. She would always tell me afterwards. *I just introduced her to them!*

Yes! Finding her was a triumph! Don't you remember, Lúcio, what a torment my life was? Have you forgotten? I could never be anyone's friend . . . I could never feel affection. Everything in me turned to tenderness. And when confronted with someone towards whom I felt that tenderness, I was filled by the desire to caress them, to possess them – in order to *satisfy* my feelings of tenderness, to make my friendships whole . . .'

A brilliant flash of flame-red light blinded my soul.

Ricardo went on:

'You have no idea how I suffered. You offered me a great affection. I wanted to feel that affection of yours, that is, to reciprocate it, but I couldn't. Only by kissing you, embracing you, possessing you. But how can one possess a creature of one's own sex?

It was terrible, terrible! I saw your friendship, saw it clearly, and yet I couldn't feel it! It was like fool's gold.

One night, though, one fantastic sleepless night, I finally succeeded! I found Her, yes, I created Her, *created* Her. She is mine alone, do you understand? Mine alone. We understand each other so completely that Marta is like a part of my own soul. We think the same way, we feel the same way. We are Us. And from that night I could feel, really feel, your affection for me vibrate inside me, I could reciprocate your affection by ordering Her to be yours! *But when she embraced you, it was me embracing you.* I satisfied my love for you. I won! And when I possessed her, I felt that I possessed *in her* the friendship I owed to you, the way others feel their affections in their souls. When I found her, you see, it was as if my soul, by becoming sexualised, had become matter. *And thus I possessed you physically with my spirit!* That is my triumph . . . my insuperable triumph! My magnificent secret!

... ...

Oh, but the pain I feel today . . . the lacerating pain I feel again today.

You judged me so unfairly . . . You were angry . . . you cried out against my shamelessness, my baseness . . . and my pride grew with every day that dawned! You fled and the truth is that you fled out of jealousy. You were not my only friend . . . you were the first, the greatest, but I also felt tenderness for another. So I sent her off to embrace that other . . . it was Warginsky, yes, you're right, Warginsky. I thought he was such a good friend . . . he seemed so spontaneous, so loyal, so worthy of my affection. And I was wrong, quite wrong.'

Astonished, I listened to Ricardo as if hypnotised, struck dumb with horror, unable to utter a word.

His pain was so real, his repentance so sincere, and I noticed that his tone of voice changed, grew lighter when he spoke of the Russian count, only to deepen again afterwards.

'But what do the others matter compared with your friendship? Nothing! Nothing! You don't believe me? Oh, but you must believe me . . . you must understand me . . . Come! She is mine alone! But for your affection I would give away everything – *even my secret*. Come!'

What happened next was pure madness.

He grabbed me violently by the arm, forcing me to run along behind him.

... ...

At last we reached his house. We went in and raced up the stairs.

As we crossed the first floor landing, an insignificant detail caught my eye and, for some reason, I have never forgotten it. On the sideboard, where the servants usually left the correspondence, was a letter. It was a large envelope bearing a gold coat of arms.

It's odd that at such a climactic moment, I should notice something as small as that. But the fact is that the gold coat of arms danced wildly before my eyes. I could not see its exact design, I could see only that it was a coat of arms and yet, at the same time – and this was even stranger – *it seemed to me that I myself had received an envelope just like that.*

My friend – though still in the grip of intense emotion – opened the letter, read it quickly, screwed it up and threw it to the floor.

Then he grasped my arm even harder.

Around me everything was shaking . . . I felt my body and soul dissolving in the whirlwind whistling about me . . . I was afraid I had fallen into the hands of a madman.

And in a voice grown still lower, still stranger, still falser – I mean simply that it seemed to issue forth from someone else's throat – Ricardo shouted to me wildly:

'Come on! It's time to rid ourselves of ghosts. She is yours alone, yours alone . . . you must believe me! I tell you again, it was as if my soul had become sexualised, as if my soul had become flesh in order to possess you . . . She is mine alone, mine alone! I only sought her out because of you . . . But I won't allow her to separate us . . . You'll see, you'll see!'

And in the midst of these incoherent, *impossible* words, he dragged me with him and ran in a fury towards his wife's apartments, which were on the second floor.

(A curious detail: at the time I did not feel that his words were impossible. I merely thought them full of a terrible anxiety . . .)

We had arrived. Ricardo gave the door a brutal shove. It opened.

Marta was standing by a window on the other side of the room, leafing through a book.

The unfortunate woman barely had time to turn round. Ricardo pulled out a revolver he had concealed in his jacket pocket and, before I could do anything, before I could make a move, he fired on her at point-blank range.

Marta fell senseless to the floor. I had not moved from where I stood on the threshold.

And then the Mystery happened . . . the fantastic Mystery of my life.

To my amazement, to my grief, *the person lying stretched out by the window was not Marta, no, it was my friend, it was Ricardo. And at my feet, yes, at my feet, lay his revolver, still smoking!*

Marta had vanished, silently evaporated, like a flame being extinguished.

Terrified, I let out an awful cry – a loud, lacerating cry – and seized by fear, my eyes bulging, my hair on end, I raced madly along corridors, through rooms, down stairways.

Then the servants came.

... ...
... ...

When I could think again, when I could put my ideas together, in short, when I awoke from that terrible, frantic nightmare, which, however unlikely, was, in fact, reality, I found myself in a cell in a State prison, watched over by a guard.

VIII

There remains little more for me to say. I could even stop my confession here. I will, however, add just a few more words.

I will pass rapidly over the trial. Nothing worth describing happened during it. For my part, I did not even attempt to establish my innocence of the crime of which I was accused. No one can justify the impossible. And so I kept silent.

My lawyer put forward a truly brilliant case. It must be said that, basically, the real culprit of my crime was Marta, who had disappeared and whom the police, I believe, had sought in vain.

People doubtless thought reasons of passion lay behind the crime. My enigmatic pose seemed most romantic. A vague air of mystery hovered over everything. Hence the jury's benevolence.

I should, however, emphasise that I have only very vague memories of my trial. My whole life had crumbled the moment Ricardo's revolver fell at my feet. Confronted with such an extraordinary secret, I plunged into the void. What did I care for what went on up above, on the surface? Prison seemed to me to offer an opportunity for rest, an ending.

That's why I saw the long, tedious hours spent in court as if through a fog, as if superimposed one on top of the other, *being played out on a stage that wasn't quite the one on which such hours should have been spent*.

Inevitably, my 'friends' vanished, including Luís de Monforte, who had so often declared his friendship for me, and Narciso de Amaral, in whose affection I had also believed. Whilst the trial was on, not one of them sent word or came to visit me, *to raise my spirits*. Not that anything could have raised my spirits.

I did, however, find a true friend in my defence lawyer.

I've forgotten his name now. I remember only that he was young and bore a remarkable physical resemblance to Luís de Monforte.

Later, at the hearings, I noticed too that the judge who questioned me was a little like the doctor who had treated me, eight years before, for a brain fever that had brought me to death's door.

It's odd how our spirit, capable of cutting off from everything at certain decisive moments, can still remember tiny details like that.

As I said before, my ten years in prison passed swiftly.

Moreover, life in the prison where I carried out my sentence was not particularly hard. The months flowed by in calm uniformity.

There was a large enclosure where, at certain times, we were allowed to walk, always watched by the guards, who mingled with us and sometimes spoke to us.

The enclosure was bounded by a large wall, a high, thick wall that faced onto a wide road or, rather, onto a sort of square crossed by several streets. Opposite – a detail that remains engraved on my memory – there was a yellow-painted barracks (or it may have been another prison).

The greatest pleasure of certain inmates was to lean over this great wall and look out at the road, at life. But the moment the jailers saw them, they would tell them brusquely to withdraw.

I rarely approached the wall, except when one of the other prisoners, using grand, mysterious gestures, beckoned me over there, for nothing on the other side held any interest for me.

In fact, I could not help a dry shudder of fear whenever I leaned over the wall or when I saw some figure high up – black, lizard-like, skeletal – pressed against the scant traces of the wall's faded yellow paint.

I never had any reason to complain about the guards, unlike some of my companions, who would recount in a low voice the ill treatment they had received.

But the truth is that sometimes, far off, you would suddenly hear strange cries – muffled at first, then loud. And one day a mulatto prisoner – doubtless a fantasist – told me that they had beaten him mercilessly with terrible scourges – *cold like ice water*, he had added in his pidgin tongue.

Besides, I mixed with very few of the other prisoners. They clearly had little to recommend them, being creatures without learning or culture, coming no doubt from the lower depths of vice and crime.

The only person I enjoyed talking to, when we were allowed out to walk round the enclosure, was a blond young man, very distinguished-looking, tall and lean. He told me that he too was in prison for a murder. He had killed his lover: a famous French singer he had brought to Lisbon.

Life had stopped for him as it had for me, he too had experienced that *culminating moment* I referred to in my introduction. In fact we often spoke of those extraordinary moments and he would talk then of the possibility of fixing, of *keeping* the most beautiful moments of our lives – ablaze with either love or fear – and thus be able to see them and feel them again. He told me that this was his one obsession in life – *his art*.

Listening to him, the novelist in me awoke again. One could write so beautifully on that disturbing topic.

But I do not want to write any more about my life in prison, which is of no interest to others, nor even to myself.

The years flew by. Touched by my serenity, my resignation to my fate, everyone treated me with great kindness and regarded me with affection. The governors themselves, who often called us to their offices or visited our cells, to talk and ask us questions, were most attentive to me.

Then the final day of my sentence arrived and the doors of the prison opened.

As if dead, without even glancing about me, I fled at once to this country retreat, isolated and remote, which now I will never again leave.

I feel quite calm, I have no desires, no hopes. I don't think about the future. My past, when I look back on it, appears to me to belong to someone else. *I am still here, but I am no longer myself.* And until my real death, all that remains for me is to watch the hours slipping past. *Real death* will merely mean a deeper sleep.

Before that, though, I wanted to write an honest account of my strange adventure, keeping it as simple as possible. It shows how the facts that seem most clear-cut to us are often the most complex; it shows how an innocent man is often unable to speak up for himself, because what he has to say is impossible, *albeit true*.

Thus, in order to be believed, I had first, in silence, to pay for a crime I did not commit.

Ah, life . . .

1–27 September 1913 – Lisbon